"Gideon, do you smell
Beth sniffed again. Her face paled.
"I smell smoke."

He sniffed, his muscles tightening. "I do. It's close."

He ran to the door and felt it. "The door is not hot. We can go out here, but stay close to me."

He pulled the door. Nothing happened. The knob wouldn't turn.

They were trapped inside the room while something burned.

Gideon spun away from the door and sprinted to the window on the side of the *haus* facing the auction barn. Flames climbed up the trellis, licking at the base of the window. Beyond the flames, he saw the cause of the suspicious fire. A man with a thick black beard hightailed it back to his motorcycle, a gas can in one beefy hand. The can sloshed fuel over the grass as he ran.

They'd been locked inside a burning *haus*.

The man who had shot Amos Troyer was attempting to roast them to death.

Dana R. Lynn grew up in Illinois. She met her husband at a wedding and told her parents she'd met the man she was going to marry. Nineteen months later, they were married. Today, they live in rural Pennsylvania with their three children and a variety of animals. In addition to writing, she works as a teacher for the deaf and hard of hearing, and is active in her church.

Books by Dana R. Lynn

Love Inspired Suspense

Amish Country Justice

Visit the Author Profile page at LoveInspired.com for more titles.

Amish Witness to Murder

DANA R. LYNN

LOVE INSPIRED SUSPENSE
INSPIRATIONAL ROMANCE

LOVE INSPIRED SUSPENSE
INSPIRATIONAL ROMANCE

Recycling programs
for this product may
not exist in your area.

ISBN-13: 978-1-335-59811-0

Amish Witness to Murder

Copyright © 2024 by Dana Roae

For questions and comments about the quality of this book, please contact us
at CustomerService@Harlequin.com.

® is a trademark of Harlequin Enterprises ULC.

Love Inspired
22 Adelaide St. West, 41st Floor
Toronto, Ontario M5H 4E3, Canada
www.LoveInspired.com

Printed in Lithuania

MIX
Paper | Supporting
responsible forestry
FSC® C021394

I called upon the Lord in distress:
the Lord answered me, and set me in a large place.
The Lord is on my side; I will not fear:
what can man do unto me?
—*Psalms* 118:5–6

This book is dedicated to the memory
of my dad, Bruce (1936–2001),
and my father-in-law, Roger (1943–2023).
Both men presented me with daily examples
of what gentleness, generosity, strength and joy
looked like. I am so grateful for your presence
in my life and will miss you every day.

ONE

She should have been home an hour ago.

Grimacing, Beth Troyer flicked the reins to coax the elderly mare from a plodding walk to a trot. She was on the way home from town to fix lunch for her father when she heard the familiar sirens coming her way. Two minutes later, the first emergency response vehicle crested the hill behind her, blasting its horn in warning. Clicking her tongue, she gripped the reins tighter in her hands and slowed the buggy before she steered the faithful family mare to the side of the road. Obediently, the animal plodded to the shoulder. The wheels of the buggy sank into the wet ground. The official start of spring was still a week away and they'd already had a record amount of rain. The air was thick with the scent of sodden earth. Several of the storms had been so bad, there had been widespread power outages and some property damage, including uprooted trees. Not to mention the flooding of ponds and creeks.

Jenny, as she secretly called the gentle horse due to her father's belief that animals shouldn't be named, stood quietly, not even flinching when the pickup truck with a blue light swirling on its roof whipped past her. The buggy shuddered in its wake.

I wonder what the emergency is.

Out of habit, she whispered a soft prayer for whoever needed assistance. The familiar ritual was as comfortable as a pair of well-worn boots. She barely even thought about what she was doing before the words sprang to her lips. It might have been a habit, but the prayers were heartfelt. Tragedy struck every day, and no one was immune.

If that weren't the case, her mother would have still been with them.

A loud, ear-piercing blare answered her silent question. A fire truck was on the way. She kept the buggy where it was, knowing she'd have to pull over again before the horse could work its way back to a full trot. Sure enough, less than a minute later, a fire truck belonging to the Sutter Springs, Ohio, volunteer fire department zoomed past, its tires spitting gravel and specks of mud against the shield in the front of the buggy. The gritty substance pinged as it struck the metal sides of the Amish vehicle.

Once she was sure all the emergency vehicles had passed, she maneuvered the buggy back onto the two-lane road and continued home. Hopefully, she would arrive before her *daed* began wondering what was keeping her. She had unexpectedly run into her friend Diana, whom she hadn't seen in weeks. Beth had delayed her return in order to see the woman's month-old daughter. Beth loved *kinder*. The biggest wound of her single state was that she had no *bopplin* of her own. By the time she had packed her groceries into the buggy and headed back toward home, she was an hour behind schedule. *Daed* tended to worry, especially since her older sister, Miriam, had up and left the family two years ago for an *Englischer*. She'd gone to her sister's room one morning to wake her for breakfast and had found the bedroom window wide open and a short note on the bedside table explaining she was done with the Amish way of life and was leaving with an *Englischer* she'd been seeing. No forwarding address had been provided. Typical of her selfish sibling. It had been just Beth and her father ever since. Their mother had died right before Beth turned two, leaving the grieving widower with two *kinder* to raise alone. He'd been a *gut daed*, although somewhat strict. She had often wondered why he hadn't remarried. Most Amish men would have, especially if they were raising *kinder* alone.

They'd had no contact with Miriam after she left. Until today. Beth glanced down at the letter she'd plucked from the mailbox before she'd left for town.

Miriam wanted to *cumme* home. She didn't say if she wanted to *cumme* to stay or merely to visit. Beth didn't know how to feel about that. Her sister had caused so many problems in the past. She wasn't sure she knew how to respond. Normally, Beth would have had no issue with giving the letter to her father and letting him make the call. He was the head of their family, after all. However, she hesitated. Her father had always seemed so strong and larger than life to her. These past few weeks, though, he'd acted as if a heavy burden was weighing him down. He wouldn't speak of his concerns with her. In his mind, she understood, she was still a little one, and not a full-grown woman. Regardless of the fact that she would be twenty-eight in less than a month.

As she moved along, she frowned.

Why weren't the sirens fading? Those vehicles were so much faster than her horse-drawn buggy. She shouldn't still be able to hear them. But hear them, she could. In fact, it seemed the sirens were getting louder. As if the trucks had reached their destination and had stopped moving. She wasn't comforted. The fire was nearby.

A thread of anxiety slid through her. One of her friends or neighbors could be in trouble. Sutter Springs was something of a tourist attraction for those curious about the Amish way of life. The entire town was a mix of *Englisch* and Amish living side by side. *Englisch* neighbors bookended her own *haus*.

Clutching the reins tighter in her fists, she flicked them, urging the mare into an extended trot. It was as fast as she dared push the animal, both because of the wet, slick roads and because she didn't want to injure Jenny. She may have been a work horse, but Beth had grown very fond of her since they'd first purchased her ten years ago.

The sirens finally ceased. Fear clutched her lungs in its grip. She couldn't relax.

A brisk breeze drafted behind the shield, spraying a cool mist on her face. A whiff of smoke teased her nose, and she froze. She hadn't realized how hard she'd been hoping it was a false alarm. Jerking her head to the left, she raised her eyes to gaze over the tree line to about where eleven o'clock would be if the landscape before her were a giant clock. Dark plumes of black smoke churned in the air.

It was close. Too close.

Her stomach quivered and her muscles clenched.

Jenny trotted forward, her flanks quivering. Even she seemed to sense the wrongness in the atmosphere. Beth sucked in a deep breath to calm herself and ended up coughing, her tongue and the roof of her mouth coated with the oily smoke.

Finally, the horse reached the corner of her road. Two fire trucks, several smaller emergency vehicles and a single police cruiser lined the road. It was hard at first to tell where the fire was coming from. But she knew. In her gut, she knew it wasn't a neighbor's *haus*.

It was hers.

She would never make it to her driveway. Too many vehicles blocked her path. Not to mention all the residents emerging from their homes, mouths open in shock as they gawked. When Sharon, the young woman who lived directly across from her, met her gaze briefly and then dropped her eyes, the bottom fell out of Beth's stomach.

Pulling her horse over to the side of the road, Beth leaped down from the buggy, stumbling on the uneven ground. Righting herself, she ran toward her home. Jenny wouldn't stray. Beth rushed forward. The gaping neighbors saw her coming and parted to make way. She didn't acknowledge them. Her heart pounded in her chest. She opened her mouth and panted, desperate to get a full breath.

The smoke was heavy in the air. She kept going. Rounding her driveway, she noted with relief that the fire wasn't coming from her *haus*. Her anxiety spiked, however, when she saw it was coming from the huge barn in the next lot.

The family's auction business.

Daed. Her father was supposed to be working in the auction barn. Had he gotten out?

The members of the volunteer fire department were everywhere, focused on keeping the blaze contained to the one building. Thankfully, the ground was wet enough to keep it from spreading over the grass. The breeze, however, would be a concern. Plenty of fires were started by embers that broke free and got carried on the wind. *Englisch* and Amish volunteers worked side by side. The volunteer fire department was one place where the two cultures worked seamlessly together. The fire was fully involved. She knew at a glance the building would be a total loss.

It was only a building, she reminded herself. Property

could be replaced, structures rebuilt. No worldly trapping was worth more than a person's life.

Cutting across the lawn, she kept out of the way of the firefighters. She had to find her father.

She raced behind the firefighters and circled to the back of the building. Flames erupted from the upstairs window. She ignored them, keeping as far from the burning building as she could. Turning the corner, shock spiked through her at the sight of two men locked together in a fierce battle. She should go for help, but she couldn't leave. Her focus remained locked on the two figures ahead of her, wrestling.

A large, bearded man she'd never seen before had her father in a choke hold.

Daed was a peaceful man. He would never fight, although he struggled to free himself. Even in his struggle, he didn't strike back.

He managed to wrench himself out of the man's hold. Instead of turning to confront him, *Daed* took several steps away, his steps staggering.

He didn't move fast enough. The stranger pulled out a gun. Right in front of her eyes, before she could shout a warning, he pulled the trigger. The cacophony around them camouflaged the blast. Her father collapsed to the ground and lay still. A dark stain spread on the grass under him.

"Daed!"

Despite the chaos, the shooter heard her shout. He raised the gun a second time, but this time, when he pulled the trigger, nothing happened. She couldn't see his eyes behind the dark sunglasses, but she could feel the rage emanating from him. Beneath the cover of the beard, his lips pulled back in a snarl. She backed up, then whirled around to run away.

Something slammed against the back of her skull. Agony ripped through her. Then everything went dark.

Miriam's *haus*. Gideon Bender buried the well-known sensation of bitterness working its way into his mind. He could taste it on his tongue. But now was not the time to dwell on her betrayal. He couldn't let it matter. No matter what his former almost-fiancée had done to him, her family was innocent and needed help.

Tom, the driver, pulled in behind a familiar police cruiser and opened the door.

"Gideon! Over here!" Gideon jumped down from the passenger side of the pickup truck he'd rode to the fire in and ran across the sodden grass to where his brother-in-law, Sergeant Steve Beck, stood with the fire inspector beyond the firefighters dealing with the inferno. He grimaced. There was no way they'd be able to save the building. Fortunately, it was Tuesday. He knew from experience that Amos Troyer spent Tuesdays at the lumberyard. While fires were always horrible, this could have turned tragic had anyone been inside the barn-turned-auction-business.

Gideon jogged toward the two men, his steps slowing as he drew closer. They broke off their conversation and watched him approach, their normally friendly expressions morphed into twin masks of resolve. His brothers, Micah and Isaiah, underwent the same shift when danger showed its face. It must be something that happened when one entered law enforcement. Micah and Isaiah had both left their Amish community years ago. Micah was now a deputy US marshal. Isaiah had been lost to them for seventeen years. When he had shown up a year and a half ago, the family had been shocked to find he'd become a bounty hunter.

Now he was a married man with an adopted six-year-old son and his wife was due to have a baby in July.

All his brothers and his sister had found love and were building families. Gideon couldn't be happier for them. He loved being the fun uncle and treasured every moment with his siblings.

That didn't mean he didn't yearn for a family of his own one day. Except Miriam had destroyed that future when she'd left him and run off to marry an *Englischer*.

None of which mattered now.

He shifted his attention back to the men before him.

"*Ja?* What can I help you with?" He needed to get back to the fire. They could use every set of hands to keep it contained. His glance slid back to the structure. The auction barn was barely visible in the midst of the flames shooting upward.

Steve sighed. "The inspector here has found evidence that an accelerant was used to start this fire."

He blinked. That was the last thing he expected to hear. "Arson?"

Who would want to hurt Amos Troyer? Except for his own *daed*, Gideon had never met a better man. Or a gentler one. Plus, the poor fellow had suffered so much. "Who would burn down an Amish business? Amos didn't have any enemies."

Did he? Maybe not Amos, but he could see Miriam making enemies.

He shook the thought away, knowing it was unworthy.

"That's what we need to find out. We'll need to talk with some of the people around here." Steve rubbed the back of his neck as if it already ached. "You know that some of your neighbors are reluctant to speak with the police."

He nodded. "*Ja.* I know. We don't generally talk with outsiders about our business."

Steve winced.

"Not you. You're my brother, ain't so? But others in the community wouldn't feel that way."

Steve had brought Gideon's twin sister, Joss, back to the family. She had been abducted twenty-five years ago, and somehow, Steve had saved her and returned her. Well, he married her. And she didn't return to the Amish. But Joss was part of their family again. Gideon had become very close to his *Englisch* brother-in-law.

"I'm not looking for compliments. Though I never mind them." Steve flashed a quick grin. "What we're suggesting is that people might be more comfortable with you talking to them. Would you consider helping out? Kind of like a consultant?"

Gideon rubbed his beardless chin. It was an interesting idea. Gideon had a reputation for being a bit of a practical joker. But the truth was, he was easily bored. And when he got bored, his mind would think up ways to entertain itself. Some of these ideas had landed him in trouble over the years. He had never talked with anyone about it, not even his siblings, but he knew that if he were in the *Englisch* school system, he would have been in the accelerated or gifted classes.

A month after she'd married his brother, Isaiah, his sister-in-law, Addison, had been talking with him and had suddenly said, "Do people realize you're a genius?"

He'd thought she was teasing, the way people do, but when he'd started to make a joke, her serious expression had made the humorous remark die in his throat.

"I'm not a genius," he'd protested. It wasn't possible to talk about how intelligent he really was and sound humble, though, so he had left it there. In the Amish world, there were no perks or rewards for being the smartest in the community. In fact, their entire lifestyle was geared toward keeping any one member from standing out. It was enough that when he and *Daed* were working in the carpentry shop, *Daed* often asked Gideon to measure something or do any intricate math, knowing Gideon could eye a piece of wood or metal and accurately tell exactly how long it was and he could solve complicated equations mentally in seconds. He had never made a fuss about it, and neither had his family. Quite the opposite. He had grown used to downplaying his abilities. Having an actual label attached to them disconcerted him. To his relief, Addison had dropped the subject. But for the first time, he felt like he'd been completely seen.

A challenge like the one Steve offered now appealed to him. *"Ja.* I will help you. Let me know when."

He turned back to the disaster at hand. Gideon wasn't the only Amish man in the volunteer fire department. He and the rest of the men worked tirelessly to contain and extinguish the flames. No one went inside the building. The air stunk of smoke and ash, but the poison fumes were dispersed enough to keep anyone from inhaling too many and becoming sick or worse.

About twenty minutes after he arrived, the chief sent Gideon to check on the ground behind the barn and make sure there were no glowing embers or sparks. With a nod, he jogged around the side.

And nearly tripped over a body lying on the ground. Righting himself, he glanced down to see who he'd run into.

Stopping, Gideon's jaw dropped. Beth Troyer, Miriam's younger sister and his old school friend, lay motionless on the wet grass. His heart leaped to his throat. How long had she been lying here? Instantly, his eyes took in her color. Pale, but not bluish. That was *gut.*

Kneeling beside her, he touched the pulse point on her neck with a shaking hand. Her skin was cool, but not waxy. A thready pulse beat against his fingertips. When he removed his hand, he exclaimed. There was blood on his fingers. Leaning in, he spied a pool of it spread beneath her. She needed medical help, now. He sprang to his feet, ready to alert the chief and get an ambulance.

"Daed." Her weak voice halted him. Spinning back, he saw her eyes remained sealed shut. Had she really spoken?

He dropped beside her again. "Beth?"

Her dry lips parted slightly. *"Daed.* Check him. Hurt bad."

She fell silent again. He glanced around and noticed a second body. What was going on? Two bodies, and neither one of them inside the burning structure. That couldn't be a coincidence. He moved to Amos's crumpled form. The man lay at an unnatural angle, but Gideon had a clear view of his vacant eyes staring at nothing. He knew without touching him that they were too late. Still, he leaned down and gently placed his fingers against Amos's cold throat. Unlike his daughter, Amos had no pulse. Although cold, lividity had barely set in. He couldn't have been dead for more than half an hour, an hour at most.

What was Amos doing here on a Tuesday? It felt wrong to worry about such a thing when the man was dead. Except, had he not been here, he would still be alive.

Sighing, Gideon shrugged out of his coat and settled it over the unconscious woman. He didn't have a second covering for Amos, but it didn't matter. The man was beyond feeling the misty drizzle starting to fall.

But Beth was still alive. Although he had no idea how extensive her injuries were, she wasn't gone.

He left her to find help, running in his haste to keep her

alive, barely noticing the hissing sound as the raindrops grew heavier and hit the burning barn. Even if he hadn't told Steve he'd help already, he was determined to involve himself in the case now.

TWO

"Steve!" Gideon pounded across the lawn to his brother-in-law. Never had he been so glad the man was an *Englisch* cop. He skidded to a halt, his heels leaving ruts in the mud. "Steve! Amos Troyer is behind the barn. He's dead. And his daughter, Beth—she's hurt wonderful bad."

Steve didn't waste time asking Gideon if he was sure. He himself had taught Gideon CPR and first aid. He immediately grabbed his cell phone and dialed 911. "Sergeant Steve Beck here. I'm requesting an ambulance." His face clenched. "There's also one known fatality. Notify the coroner."

Gideon tightened his shoulders, holding the pain of the request at bay. At one time, not so long ago, he had thought Amos would one day be his father-in-law. Now he was gone, without warning. Leaving Beth completely alone in the world.

He needed to get back to her.

"Show them where to go," he told Steve.

"I should come with—"

He cut him off. "You're needed here. What if they're not the only casualties? Now that we know they were home?"

Steve pursed his lips, then nodded. "There might be others. I'll get a team searching."

Leaving Steve to direct the ambulance when it arrived, he dashed across the street to the first fire truck, opened the hatch where the emergency supplies were kept and yanked out a couple of blankets and the first aid kit. He wasn't a paramedic or a doctor, but he did know something about treating someone for shock.

He refused to consider that he might be too late to help her. Visions of Beth laughing at something he'd said, of her racing with him down the road while his brother Zeke timed them—and sometimes winning—flooded his mind. She'd been his friend for so many years. Before he had severed ties with her family.

Wincing, he cut off that line of thought. He didn't have time for memories, *gut* or bad. He raced back to Beth and dropped down near her head, his gut twisting at the sight of her pale skin. Alarm spiked through him when his eyes fell on her blue-tinged lips. They hadn't been like that when he'd left her a few minutes earlier. He placed his fingers against the side of her neck where the carotid artery was and felt for a pulse. His shoulders drooped when he felt the warmth of her neck and the beat of her heart. She was still with him.

"It's *gut,* Beth." He draped a thick blanket over her, then balled up the second one. He placed it under her calves, raising her feet slightly. He kept up a steady stream of soothing conversation. He had no idea if she could hear him. "I asked Steve to call the ambulance. Help is on the way. I'll stay here with you until it comes, okay? Your head is bleeding. I'm going to try and see where, so I can put some pressure on it, okay?"

He didn't expect a response, but when he took a clean gauze bandage and hunched over her to try to get a better view, she groaned. "Beth? Are you awake?"

She didn't answer. A groan was *gut,* though, right? She wasn't completely unconscious. At some level, she was aware of what was happening. He hoped.

Footsteps squelched up to him. Two paramedics approached, pushing a wheeled stretcher. One positioned himself across from Gideon. The other continued past him to Amos. Gideon didn't say anything, knowing they couldn't take his word that the man was dead.

The woman was back thirty seconds later and placed herself at Beth's head. "Good job covering her up and elevating her feet."

"I think she might be going into shock," Gideon informed them. "Her skin felt clammy, and she was so pale. Her pulse isn't steady either, ain't so?"

They both raised their eyebrows. "All true," the female paramedic agreed. "Has she regained consciousness at all?"

"She spoke twice. And she groaned. She didn't open her eyes, though."

He kept his eyes trained on the other paramedic who worked to stem the bleeding. It felt like an eternity before they gently hefted her to the stretcher. Gideon had hoped she would respond in some way to the movement. A word. Another groan. Anything.

There was nothing.

Gideon started to follow them to the ambulance, but the arrival of the coroner gave him pause. As much as he wanted to remain with Beth, he knew his duty, as the person who found Amos, was to remain with the coroner and answer what questions he could. It wasn't typical for members of the Amish community to be on a first name basis with the elected county coroner. However, as a volunteer fireman, Gideon was in a unique position. He had gotten to know Dane Lenz over the past three years whenever the coroner had been called to the scene of an accident or a fatal fire.

This was the first time he'd seen him at a homicide.

It hadn't been ruled as such yet, but Gideon had put the

puzzle together in his mind. The back of Amos's dark coat had flipped up as he fell, revealing his blood soaked shirt. There was nothing in the surrounding area that could have caused both Amos's death and Beth's head injury. They were deliberately inflicted. He had no doubt. He held his tongue, though, and waited for Dane to examine the body and ask questions.

"Gunshot," the coroner grunted, peering close to the dead man's back. After a few more minutes, he grunted again. "No exit wound. His death wasn't an accident."

Dane turned and squinted up at Gideon. "Steve said you found him, son. Want to tell me what happened?"

Gideon clasped his hands loosely behind his back and described stumbling over Beth and her asking him to see to her father.

Steve joined them as he was finishing his story.

"Poor Amos. Joss will be sad. She liked him."

"Ja. We all did. He was a *gut* man." Guilt pulsed in Gideon's soul. He had all but abandoned Amos and Beth after Miriam's betrayal. Prior to that, he would have assisted Amos in setting up for an auction. Could he have prevented this tragedy had he still been an active part of their lives?

Dane heaved himself to his feet. "He was shot in the back, Steve. Bullet's still in him."

The skin around Steve's eyes tightened. "We need that bullet. I want whoever did this behind bars."

"Let me get him back to the coroner office where it's dry. I'll get you that bullet. Then it'll be up to you to find out who put it there."

Steve agreed before glancing at Gideon. "The firefighters are about done. They're cleaning up now."

"That's wonderful *gut* to hear. I want to go to the hospital and see how Beth is doing. She shouldn't be alone."

"How about I give you ride?" Steve shoved his sunglasses down over his eyes. The day had started cloudy, but golden rays were now starting to peek through the clouds. "It won't take me but a moment to let the fire inspector know what I'm doing."

That was something he appreciated about Steve. He didn't ask nosy questions or read too much into things. "*Ja.* That would work."

He started to turn away, then paused. "Dane, Steve, one thing. I keep remembering that Tuesdays were always busy at the lumberyard. Amos would have been there. I don't know why he was here today. It may be so his schedule changed. I haven't spoken with him in a while." Steve rubbed the back of his head. "Well, we'll have to check in on that. If he hadn't been expected, it could have been a case of Amos interrupting something, like a robbery, or an arson attempt."

They ambled toward where Steve had parked the cruiser. "The fire inspector wants to sift through the debris, but it's too hot now. I'll be out again tomorrow to assist him."

Gideon nodded, but he wasn't really listening. His thoughts shifted to the woman he had found on the ground. The last time he'd seen Beth, tears had been streaming out of her large brown eyes as she'd told him about Miriam's betrayal. He hadn't blamed Beth or Amos. But being around them had been painful, so he had avoided them, going out of his way not to talk to Beth. She and Miriam didn't look a thing alike. Miriam had been petite and all blond sunshine and giggles. Beth was taller, her manner quiet, with warm chocolate brown eyes and deep chestnut hair. He had never heard her giggle. When she laughed, it was a full-throated laugh.

He'd seen her hurt when he'd avoided her.

Now, he admitted to himself, he had been wrong to treat one of his oldest friends so shamefully.

Hopefully, he would have the chance to gaze into her eyes and apologize. His blood went cold at the thought that he might be too late.

Beth was wrapped in cotton.

That wasn't right. She struggled to push through the grogginess that surrounded her. She knew she wasn't awake, but she wasn't fully asleep either. What had happened?

Ice clawed at her throat. She needed to wake up. Urgency pelted her mind. Something bad happened. The memory eluded her. Why was her mind so hazy? She tried to move, but her limbs seemed weighted down.

Almost as if she were drugged. She recalled a voice saying her head was bleeding. Had she been in an accident? She must be in the hospital. The edge of the panic grew tighter around her heart. She had to wake up.

Above her, disembodied voices carried on a casual conversation.

"Fran, good to see you. I didn't expect to see you here."

Fran? She didn't know anyone named Fran. The deep male voice was unfamiliar.

"Hey, Steve. I had a cancellation. When the chief said there might possibly be a witness, I thought I'd drop in and see if there were any signs that she was regaining consciousness."

"Really?" the male voice said, surprised. "You hate hospitals."

She'd been right. She was in the hospital.

"I do. But I go there if that's where my job takes me," the woman said, her tone snappy.

"Don't we all? The doctor came in ten minutes ago. He said she stirred a little and should wake up soon," the man responded. Steve, the woman said his name was. "Still, he said there was no way to know for sure. She might come out of it today, or she might not. Nothing we can do about it either way."

"She's going to wake up," a third voice growled. This voice she knew. Gideon was here? She hadn't talked with him in nearly two years. Why would he show up now? She was missing something important. She tried to force her lips open, to tell them she could hear them. They wouldn't obey. She refused to give up. She would make herself heard. Her mind seemed clearer now. The heaviness had begun to dissipate. While still bone weary, she wiggled her fingers and was positive they truly moved.

"Look!" Gideon's voice broke through, closer than before. "Her fingers are moving."

"I'll call the doctor," the other man spoke. She heard footsteps striding away from her, then the sound of a curtain being pushed aside and rattling back into place. The sound startled her. She must be in the emergency room. Last year, she'd gone with one of her friends who'd been in an accident. She recalled the curtained off cubicles. That would account for the other noises.

She tuned out the voices above her and focused on regaining control of her body.

Beth had no concept of how much time had passed when the curtain jangled again and someone entered.

"Sergeant Beck said the patient was moving," a calm voice said. The newcomer approached her. If she could open her eyes, she'd probably see him standing directly over her. That was an uncomfortable thought. She hated being so vulnerable.

"Awake," she muttered. The sound of her own voice, husky and sleepy, brought a cascade of relief.

The voices around her stilled, before they began speaking over each other. Finally, Gideon spoke next to her, his words loud and slow. "Beth? Can you hear me?"

She attempted to respond, but it felt like her mouth was stuffed with cotton. She swallowed a couple of times, hoping to get some moisture in her mouth, and tried to speak again.

"Ja. I hear you. Am I in the hospital?"

"You are," the other man responded. Sergeant Beck. That was the name the doctor had used. "Do you remember the fire?"

Fire?

A memory seared through her. She gasped, pain seizing her heart. *"Daed!"*

"I'm sorry, Beth." Gideon's voice throbbed with sorrow. That's when she knew her father hadn't survived the gunshot. Suddenly, she wished she hadn't awakened. Sleeping would be better than the agony ripping through her.

"Beth, I'm Sergeant Beck. I'm Gideon's brother-in-law. I need to know—did you see what happened?"

She recalled that Gideon's sister had returned and had married a police officer. "He was shot. A man with a long black beard shot him. He had on sunglasses." She would never forget that face. "When he came after me, I tried to run. Something struck me from behind."

"We didn't find what hit you at the scene. We'll keep looking."

"Beth, my name is Francesca Brown." The woman she'd heard talking earlier broke through her grief. "I'm a forensic artist. I work with the departments in the area. Would you be willing to work with me to make a sketch of the man? We'd have a better chance of apprehending him if his image was out there."

All she wanted was for everyone to leave so she could

mourn her father. Hot tears pressed against the inside of her eyelids. They were still too heavy to open. Maybe if she answered all their questions, they'd leave her alone.

"You would have to ask my bishop," she told the woman.

"I already did. I stopped by to discuss the issue with him before I came to the hospital. He said as long as the shooter wasn't an Amish man, I could ask for your assistance and circulate his picture."

"He wasn't Amish." In her mind, she could see the way his full beard and mustache had completely obscured his mouth. No Amish man would grow a mustache. Unlike the beards married men grew, mustaches were often identified with military figures. The Amish were absolute pacifists. "He had a mustache. I couldn't see his eyes. He was really big. Maybe two or three inches taller than my father. And muscular."

"That's good! If you work with me, we can get an image to all the precincts and people can search for him. Would you be willing to help?"

She sighed. "*Ja*. I will help." A sob burst from her throat. "He killed my *daed*."

A gentle hand landed on her shoulder. Gideon. He'd comforted her that way when they were younger. Before Miriam had destroyed their friendship.

Now she had nothing left.

Frowning in concentration, she tried to open her eyelids. It took some effort, but finally, she opened her eyes. Except…

"Why is it so dark?"

No one answered at first. Then quick footsteps moved to the bed. Gideon's hand disappeared from her shoulder.

"No reaction," the doctor said. No reaction to what?

"Miss Troyer, I'm shining a light in your eyes. What do you see?"

She flinched away from the light. She couldn't breathe. The panic took hold again. She jerked her head. "Everything is blurry. I can see shadows and light, but no faces or distinct shapes."

She heard the hysteria in her voice but could do nothing to stop it. For all intents and purposes, she was blind.

"Please don't panic," the doctor directed. "You've suffered a blow to the head. Temporary loss of vision is not unheard of."

She latched on to a single word. "Temporary? My vision will come back?"

He hesitated. "I can't promise that. However, it is very possible. I need to get an ophthalmologist here to examine you."

"When?" She'd never been *gut* at waiting.

"Dr. Lasko is out today and tomorrow. She'll be in Thursday morning. I'll have you put at the top of her caseload." The doctor's voice floated to her, devoid of any emotion. If only she could see his face!

Frustration bit at her, making her voice sharper than normal. "She'll be able to help me, ain't so?"

The answer wasn't the definitive response she craved.

"Again, I can't promise. I'll defer to the specialist."

She felt like she was wobbling on the edge of a yawning pit. She relied on her vision for everything. Driving her buggy. Reading. Sewing. Following recipes. So many things she wouldn't be able to do until it healed.

Nor would she be able to look at a drawing and identify the killer who'd left her an orphan…until her vision returned.

If her vision returned. Blood pounded in her ears. She'd never felt so helpless or alone in her life.

THREE

She couldn't see.

Gideon sank into the chair next to the hospital bed and stared at Steve, shocked. He never would have foreseen this. Oh, sure, he knew that blunt force trauma could cause the condition. When he'd joined the volunteer fire department, he'd had access to the reading materials provided for those wanting to become EMTs and paramedics. He'd read those and all the medical texts had given him an appreciation for how wonderful *gut Gott*'s creation was.

And how fragile it could be.

The ocular globe could be injured. Or a retina could be damaged. Such conditions normally didn't last long. Still, he'd never actually known of anyone who had suffered with it.

He exchanged glances with Steve. There would be no point in having her talk with Fran until her eyes healed. She'd never be able to tell Fran if the picture she created was accurate. It would do no *gut* to pass around an image if it wasn't that of the killer.

It meant they would need to wait until she got her sight back. He refused to consider that she wouldn't heal. Gideon liked to think positively. Or at least he had, until Miriam had left him devastated. It had been one loss too many.

First, his twin had vanished when he was two. Then Micah, his eldest brother, had left the family when Gideon was eleven. Two years later, his brother Isaiah had also left. Gideon and his older brother Zeke had been the only two remaining siblings at home. Reserved Zeke had responded by becoming more reserved. Gideon had become a practical joker.

He shook the morose memories aside. It had all happened years ago. Joss, Micah and Isaiah had all returned, one at a time. But Miriam's defection was permanent. Even if she had returned, he didn't know if he could forgive her.

That was not something he enjoyed admitting. He believed strongly in the need to forgive others, like Jesus had taught when he'd shown his disciples how to pray.

And yet, forgiveness was not something Gideon felt ready to extend. Because of Miriam, he'd lost the chance at marriage and family, and a lifelong friendship had ended. That part was on him, but he knew it wouldn't have happened if he hadn't been so angry and hurt. A gap he'd never experienced yawned open between himself and *Gott*. A gap he was responsible for.

Sighing, he returned his focus to the young woman on the narrow hospital cot. Gideon didn't want to leave Beth, not after what had happened to her, but when the nurse arrived, she promptly kicked everyone else out.

"I'll stop by to see you later," he promised Beth. She turned her head in his direction. Her eyes stared through him, blank. He winced and turned to leave.

"Why?"

Her husky whisper caught his attention. He halted near the edge of the curtain leading out of the small cubicle. "What do you mean?"

"You've been wonderful *gut*, taking care of me, coming

to see me. But you don't have to *cumme* back. You ended our friendship two years ago." Her matter-of-fact words couldn't hide the shade of pain tainting them. *Ja*, he'd hurt her when he'd turned his back on the Troyers. He'd never been so ashamed of his own actions as he was at this moment.

Heat scorched the back of his neck. "I shouldn't have done that. I regret it deeply. Truly. You are not your sister. I have never stopped thinking of you as a friend. I just needed some space."

It sounded weak even to his own ears.

She shrugged and turned her face to the wall.

Sighing, he followed Steve out of the hospital to his car. Regardless of what she thought, he'd still be back. Losing her as a friend was something he did not want to contemplate. He might have to eat a bit of crow, but she had always been worth it.

Steve pulled his key fob from his jacket pocket and hit the Unlock button. The locking mechanism clicked twice. Gideon opened the passenger side door and folded his five-foot-ten-inch frame into the seat. Once he had buckled himself in, he shifted to observe Steve. Grim lines were carved into his brother-in-law's face.

"What do you plan to do now?" he asked.

Steve shrugged. "We investigate like normal. Best case scenario—in a few days, we'll get the sketch. Tomorrow we'll go through the debris with the fire inspector. Maybe we'll—"

He broke off when his phone rang and jabbed the button on the dash to respond to the call. "Beck here."

"Sergeant," a smooth voice on the other end said. Gideon recognized the fire inspector, Vince McConnell. The man had a unique tone. Gideon had a knack for remembering voices. "While cleaning up after the fire had been put out, one of the men found a body in the rubble."

Gideon sat forward so fast he nearly smacked his head on the roof of the cruiser.

Steve whistled. "Any idea whose body they recovered?"

"Unknown. The coroner has been called to the scene for the second time. He's at another call, so he won't be here for another hour or so. The crime scene people will hang out until he gets here. The body is in very rough condition. All we know is it was a male. His own mother wouldn't recognize him."

"I'll go through the missing persons file, but it's possible he hasn't been reported missing yet. So, we'll need the coroner's report to identify him."

"I understand. Just thought you'd like to be kept in the loop. I still plan on searching through the debris tomorrow. Should I call you after the coroner leaves?"

Steve tapped his fingers on the steering wheel. "No. Listen, I need to talk with someone, but then I will come back to the scene. Maybe if Dane is still there, I can see him and the body tonight."

"I'll let them know."

He disconnected the call.

"I wonder if the dead man was killed by the fire," Gideon muttered, thinking it was unlikely.

Steve spared him a quick glance. "You and I are on the same page. I think it's curious that a body shows up in the wake of a fire where another man is gunned down. Too coincidental."

A second murder. Gideon felt the horror of it deep in his soul. He'd seen ugly things in his life. One never got used to them, though.

Steve turned off the engine. "I need to speak with Beth again ASAP."

ASAP turned out to be an hour later. She had been moved to a double occupancy room and was sitting up in the hospital bed, her lovely eyes covered with thick gauze bandages, her prayer *kapp* perched on top of her rich brown hair. She turned her head at their approach.

Gideon ignored the other patient in the room, who stared at them with avid interest.

"Told you I'd be back," Gideon quipped, then winced. Now was not the time for humor.

The corners of her lips curled upward. "*Ja*, you did. According to the nurse, you and the police officer have been waiting for a little while."

"Beth, this is Steve Beck, Joss's husband."

She dipped her head, regal despite the bandages. "I remember."

"Ma'am, I hate to bring you more bad news," Steve began, pitching his voice low to keep their conversation private, "but do you know of anyone else who might have been at your father's auction business today?"

She tilted her head. "*Nee*. It's Tuesday. He had a mud sale scheduled for Saturday. Everything was ready for it. *Daed* was wonderful worried about it."

"Why?" Gideon frowned. "I have *cumme* to several of his auctions. They always bring in a crowd and run smoothly."

Actually, his mud shows, or auctions, typically brought in crowds of several hundred. People all over the district donated items to sell. Amos would have been one of several auctioneers selling the items.

She shrugged. "I'm not sure. I think someone he was working with was being difficult."

"I remembered that he always worked at the lumberyard on Tuesdays." Gideon said, broaching the subject gently.

"*Ja*, that used to be so. Until about four months ago. Then he changed his days. He never said why. I was supposed to bring him lunch today. I was late getting home." A sudden sob welled up and burst from her throat. "Maybe if I'd been on time—"

"Stop." Without thinking, he reached out and touched her arm. She shook his hand off. Ouch. "You can't know that."

"Ma'am," Sergeant Beck's voice intervened. "Your being late might be the reason you're alive. You are our one hope to finding whoever did this."

She nodded, obviously struggling for control.

"Who was the auction for?" Steve asked.

Gideon smirked. Steve had learned a lot about the Amish in the past few years, but still had much to learn. "You're thinking of *Englisch* auctions, which are normally held when someone dies."

"*Ja,*" Beth jumped in. "Amish hold mud sales each spring and many members contribute. It's a fun event. Perfect for a tourist town."

Steve let out a heavy breath, obviously disappointed. "Well, hopefully we'll know more tomorrow after the inspection."

He stood to leave.

Gideon remained seated. He had another question. "How long will you be in the hospital?"

"I can leave tomorrow morning. They said I need to be observed."

"Will you go back to your *haus*?" Even with the top half of her face covered, he could see she'd lost color.

She heaved a gusty sigh, and her head appeared to sink

farther into the nearly flat hospital pillow. "I don't know. My mind is wonderful muddled right now."

He understood. How could she return to the home when her father was murdered at the barn next to the *haus*? He should ask her to *cumme* home and stay with his family. They had a large *haus*. It seemed so much grander now that only he and his parents lived there. There'd be plenty of room for her to stay without cramping their style, as Micah would say.

But...

It had been so long since they'd talked. The connection they'd once shared had been severed, and while Miriam's betrayal had been the catalyst, his own actions condemned him. Worse, he knew he'd been more than slightly hypocritical. He'd lectured all three of his older brothers when they were making dumb relationship decisions. Then he'd abandoned Beth. Her family had already suffered more than enough heartache. For all his intelligence, he'd still messed up.

She looked so small and frail in the hospital bed. And he didn't remember her having anyone else to turn to. He couldn't just leave her.

He leaned closer to the bed and placed his hand on the side rail. "Beth, *cumme* stay with my family. Please. Let *Mamm* spoil you while you plan your father's funeral and the police try to find those responsible."

Indecision flittered across her face. She had always enjoyed her independence. And it had to rankle—the thought of relying on him after he'd all but abandoned her. He didn't press. Beth was old enough to make her own choices.

He sent up a silent prayer. If she stayed under their roof, he'd be able to watch over her better. Because someone had killed her father and a stranger. That same person had left her for dead. He wasn't convinced she'd be safe once the killer realized the woman he'd left lying in the rain was still breathing.

Cumme stay with his family? Beth knew that Gideon's siblings had all left home. It would be his *mamm*, his *daed*. And Gideon. No one else in the home.

Beth squirmed on the uncomfortable hospital cot. She'd never appreciated the advantages of her sight until it was gone. Gideon had one of those faces that held nuances in every expression. If only she could see him. She might be able to decipher what he was truly thinking. Did he really want her, Miriam's sister, in his home? Or was he offering from a place of obligation? She had heard regret threaded through his words earlier. Although she was not sure what he regretted. Walking away? Or did he wish he'd never had anything to do with her family?

What should she do? One thought took precedence over all the others. She could not return to her home. Not now, when her *daed* wouldn't be there. Would never be there again. She shuddered, her mind swimming in grief. Her father was all she had left in the world and now he was gone. How did she even begin to process life without his presence? It wasn't like when her mother had died. She'd been so young. She had no memory of her mother being at home. Being Amish, there were no pictures to remind her of what her *mamm* had looked like. Her *daed* had never talked about her. Miriam had talked about their mother a few times over the years, but once Miriam had shown her true colors and started flirting with anyone her friends or Beth had shown interest in, Beth had stopped trusting her with her innermost thoughts. Then Miriam had gone too far and had deliberately gone after the one man Beth had ever truly been interested in, and any relationship the sisters possessed had been destroyed.

And now that man was next to her hospital bed, offering her a place to stay. If only she could see him. Frustrated, the back of her eyes stung. Sorrow mixed with bitterness welled up inside her, nearly choking her.

Another thought tugged at her mind.

"Sergeant Beck?"

"Yes, ma'am?" The deep timbre of the police officer's voice answered her.

"My *haus*… I can't go there now, can I?"

"Right now, your house, and the auction barn, are both part of an active crime scene. The fire is being investigated, as is your father's murder."

Murder. She winced. Her stomach twisted and churned. She fought back the urge to gag. If she had eaten lunch, it wouldn't have stayed down. She couldn't wrap her head around it. Someone had deliberately killed her *daed*, and she had seen it happen. She would never forget how fast he dropped to the ground.

Suddenly, it was too much. There were so many people in her room, crowding into her personal space. All she wanted was to weep herself into oblivion, to mourn the only parent she'd ever known.

Mourning, however, was a luxury she didn't have. She had never planned a funeral before. The community would rally around and help her, she knew, but the thought of going through her *daed*'s things, of trying to make decisions alone, overwhelmed her. And then there was the man who had attacked her and killed *daed*. Had he also been responsible for the other man's death? The fact that someone would be able to casually destroy so many lives whirled through her like a flood. She'd not encountered such evil before. The police would be searching for him.

Why her father?

The question swam inside her mind. He had been a quiet man, observing all but saying little. But always the first to lend a hand.

Would his killer seek her out? He'd stared directly into her eyes and had tried to shoot her. If she regained her sight, she would be able to identify him. Obviously, he wanted her dead. But did he know that Amish people rarely involved the *Englisch* police?

Probably not. Otherwise, why shoot *Daed*? Grief swamped her again. Beth swallowed, hard. The bitter lump in her throat went down like a rock. She drew in a deep breath, then released it on a shaky exhale.

"Beth? What do you say? Will you *cumme* home with me?"

Gideon's voice jarred her from her thoughts. Biting back the angry words on the tip of her tongue, she forced herself to take a deep breath before responding.

It would be so easy to accept. She'd have a refuge. But at what cost? Gideon's *haus* might be safer, but would she be bringing danger to his family? And not only that, could she risk trusting him again? *Ja*, that was a huge stumbling block, because Gideon had failed her before. She hadn't appreciated being thrown over as if she were nothing compared to her sister. Of course, she had grown used to people not noticing her when Miriam was around. Beth had always been tall and wiry. And strong. As a *kind*, she'd become the *sohn* her father had always wanted. Beth had learned to do barn chores without complaining. People often commented on how much she looked like *Daed*. Same brown eyes and the chestnut hair peeking out from under her prayer *kapp* was directly from him.

Miriam, on the other hand, resembled their mother, or so Miriam had told her. Small, a full four inches shorter than Beth, with pale golden hair and blue eyes that she used well. Miriam looked like the picture of a sweet ingenue one often saw on the Amish romances lining the shelves in the book section of the local big box store.

Her heart, though, had been selfish and cold. For years, Beth had been the only one who knew how scheming her sister had been. Miriam had hidden her discontent from everyone else. Beth understood why her sister had confided in her. It wasn't because of sisterly affection. *Nee.* Miriam had shown her nothing but scorn the last year before she'd left.

Most people didn't even realize that Miriam was the reason that Beth remained unmarried.

She jerked her mind away from that path. She had forgiven that sin long ago. It did no *gut* to dwell on it now.

But she hadn't forgotten it.

Nor had she forgotten Gideon's part in it.

Another thought struck. He had no idea that Miriam had contacted her. What would he say? She didn't want to tell him.

Which was why she couldn't accept Gideon's offer now. She had already learned that he could be turned away. She needed someone she could rely on if she were to get through this current tragedy.

"I'll be *gut*," she informed him. "I have friends I can stay with. Don't worry about me."

It was true. She had friends. *Daed* had been well respected.

She didn't like the idea of burdening anyone with her problems. Or bringing trouble into anyone's home. Well, she'd have to. Sending up a quick prayer, she begged *Gott* to shine a little light on her situation. And please, let her sight return.

Next to the bed, fabric rustled. Like someone shifted in discomfort.

"Beth," Gideon began. She pressed her lips together and glared in what she hoped was his direction. He halted whatever argument he had begun to make. Sighed. "Fine. If that's what you want to do. But don't forget my *haus* is an option, if nothing else works out, okay?"

"I won't. But *denke*." The urge to be sarcastic, to let him know how she really felt, raged inside. She fought it down and kept her voice calm and neutral. As if they were acquaintances and didn't have an ugly past between them.

Always be polite, her father would tell her, *even when you want to scream.*

There was a second or two of silence before she heard the distinct sound of footsteps edging away from the bed. Gideon murmured a quiet farewell. At least he hadn't said something inane such as *gut to see you*. When the door closed behind Gideon and Steve, she drew in a deep breath.

Finally. They were gone.

A sob took her by surprise.

It was so dark, and she was all alone. Beth gave in to her grief. Would her world ever be right again?

FOUR

"There's nothing you can do about it, man," Steve told him for the third time as they settled into the Sutter Springs police cruiser. One thing he appreciated about his brother-in-law—the man never seemed to lose his patience.

"I know that!" Gideon repeated, his voice a little sharper than it had been the first two times he had said it. "I know I can't make her stay with my family. I don't have to like it. I know the family, Steve. Beth has no other relatives in the area. Who will she stay with? *Nee*, I don't like it at all."

That was putting it mildly. It was a wonderful bad idea, leaving her alone in the hospital.

"I get it." Steve left it there and backed out of his space.

"What if the killer looks for her? She's there without a guard. No one to protect her." The thought made him want to hop out of the cruiser and run back to the hospital to make sure she was *gut*. "She can't even see. She's vulnerable now, ain't so?"

Steve rubbed the back of his neck. "Gideon, I understand you're worried about your friend. Would it help if I told you I had a chat with hospital security before we left? They are putting someone on the room."

He hadn't known that. "Well." He dragged out the word

as he considered it closely. "I guess that works. I know the police department is stretched right now."

One of the lieutenants that had helped Joss several years ago, Lieutenant Nicole Quinn, was off on maternity leave. Her partner, Lieutenant Kathy Bartlett, was testifying at court for the next few days and wouldn't be available. That's what happened in a small department in rural Ohio.

He sighed. There was nothing else to be done. Steve had, as usual, done his due diligence and made sure the victim was as safe as he could reasonably make her. The only thing better would be if she would cease being stubborn and agree to *cumme* stay with his family.

He knew better than to say it out loud for the fourth time.

Steve put his left blinker on. Gideon raised his eyebrows. "Obviously, you're not driving me home first."

Shaking his head, Steve spun the wheel in his hands and turned. "Sorry. I should have asked first, but I have to go back to the crime scene. I don't have time to drop you off at your house on the way."

"That's fine. I don't mind going with you." Actually, Gideon wouldn't have gone home. He wasn't a police officer, but a *gut* friend—former friend—was in the hospital and her father was dead. He wasn't going to pretend nothing was wrong.

A tiny voice in his mind whispered that had he not left Beth to deal with the fallout of Miriam's departure alone, then maybe she'd let him in to assist her now. He wasn't arrogant enough to think he could have done anything to prevent the current situation. However, if he had continued to be a frequent guest at the Troyer family home, it wouldn't have been outside the realm of possibilities that he may have observed something out of place.

"Stop, Gideon," Steve ordered. The cruiser came to a stop at a red light.

"What?" He raised his eyebrows in his brother-in-law's direction.

Steve gave him a quick frown. The light switched to green, and Steve continued driving. "I can tell you're beating yourself up about Beth's situation. Stop. Anything in the past is unchangeable. The future is still unknown. And I have a body waiting for us that might give us some information. Let's not borrow trouble."

Easy for him to say.

Gideon held his silence. Steve was a *gut* police officer. He adored Gideon's twin sister and treated her well. That meant a lot to Gideon. To his entire family. He barely remembered the time when Joss had been stolen from their family when she and Gideon were two years-old. Back then, she was known as Christina. Twenty-two years later, she'd found her family again. Gideon hadn't remembered her, but he'd always felt like a part of him was missing. When she had rejoined the family, the connection between them had been immediate.

Five minutes later, Steve steered the cruiser into the Troyer's driveway. The acrid smoke continued to pour from the destroyed structure. Ash coated the yard and the vehicles lining the property. The fire inspector remained on the scene. The coroner had returned as well. He could see other professionals walking along the property. Those must be the crime scene people the other officer had mentioned.

Gideon sat straight in his seat. Despite the tragic events of the day, his interest was stirred.

Steve shut off the engine. "This won't be good."

Gideon exited the vehicle when Steve did. The other man didn't even attempt to tell him to remain in the cruiser. They made their way over to where the coroner was finishing up with a blackened lump on the ground. Gideon swallowed hard. That was all that had been left of a body. Dane zipped the body bag and instructed that it be carried to his vehicle. Then he turned to the team surrounding him.

"I'm sure you've all guessed, but that body wasn't there by accident. I will have to run tests and do an autopsy, but the fire inspector agrees with me. That body was the source of the fire that burned the barn down."

Gideon blinked. He hadn't expected that. "Is the body covered with some kind of accelerant?"

The coroner nodded. "From the amount of damage to where the body was and the burn patterns on the ground, it's pretty clear to me that the accelerant, probably gasoline, was poured over the poor soul found in there. The rest of the barn went quickly."

"Because of all the flammable items for the auction," Gideon concluded.

The fire inspector concurred. "We'll see if we can have an arson dog brought in to verify, but I'm convinced. The fire in the auction barn was intentional."

Steve hissed. "The victim was dead before the fire started."

Dane sighed. "We hope. Anyways, he didn't die naturally."

"How can you tell it was a male?" From where he stood, the body was too charred to see any distinguishable features.

"I don't know for sure. I won't know for sure until I see the dental records. However, a toupee was found near the entrance. None of the Amish would wear one, and none of the law enforcement crawling over the grounds do. So, my guess? It's either from the killer or the victim."

"It might have DNA," Steve mused.

"That's definitely a possibility."

Two murders on the same property. Gideon shook his head. "Will you be able to identify him or her?"

"If the teeth are still intact or if there's DNA, yes. It might take some time. But yes, we will be able to identify the person if they're in our system at all."

Steve stepped away to call his chief. A moment later, he motioned Gideon over. "Since there have already been two murders and one attempted murder on this property—" Gideon tried not to wince at the mention of the attacks on Beth and her father "—we don't need a warrant to search the house for any evidence regarding the case."

"We?"

Steve nodded. "It's not normal procedure, but you know the family. It's possible you might notice something out of place that I would miss."

He couldn't protest. Even though he hadn't *cumme* to visit the family, he had been inside their *haus* a few times since Miriam left. Their district held church every two weeks. Each time, it was held in the home of one of the families. Although he hadn't been inside all the rooms, he'd seen more than Steve.

It was worth trying.

The back door of the *haus* was unlocked. As they entered the kitchen through the mudroom, Gideon knew immediately that something was off.

"Amos and Beth are both organized and orderly," he informed Steve, scanning the chaotic mess of items strewn on the countertops. Two of the kitchen drawers were partially opened. Someone had gone through them. "They'd never leave this kind of clutter for anyone to see."

Steve's mouth tightened, but he only nodded. Room by room, it was the same story. When they went upstairs to the bedrooms, anger began to burn in Gideon's gut. What kind of person would go through Beth's things and leave her room a wreck?

For that was the only way to describe it. The china she'd had on her dresser had been viciously smashed to pieces. Every year, an Amish girl was given a piece or two of the set so when she married, she'd have a full set of dishes. Beth had never married, and she was older than most Amish girls when they entered that state of life, but those dishes represented years of her life. Her hopes and dreams. He knew that she had to have picked the colors. Unsurprisingly, lavender and purple were everywhere in her room.

And someone had destroyed it. Even the faceless Amish doll on her bed had been sliced open.

"What were they looking for?" Steve muttered.

"This doesn't look like sheer maliciousness to you?"

"That does." Steve pointed to the shattered china. "The rest looks like someone was trying to find something. I'd guess they got very angry because they couldn't find it and destroyed the dishes."

Gideon's jaw hardened. "I don't care what she says. She can't stay unprotected at a friend's *haus*."

Steve looked at him.

"Please, can we go back to the hospital? I want to try and change her mind. At my *haus*, even if you can't stay there, between you, Micah and Isaiah, we can think of a plan. Some way to keep Beth safe."

He didn't know how he'd convince her, but he had to. If he didn't, she might end up like her *daed*—dead.

A soft knock on her door woke Beth from the light doze she'd fallen into. Startled, she jolted upright. At first, she was confused by the dark. Then the memories rushed in on her again. She groaned. She had no idea what time of day or night it was. All she knew was she was alone in this world and the man who had murdered her sweet *daed*, who had never said a cross word to anyone, had also tried to end her life.

The door creaked slightly as it was pushed open.

"Beth? Are you awake?" a too-familiar voice hissed.

Gideon. Why did her pulse jump? And there lay more heartache. Tempted to pretend she couldn't hear him, she rose above the urge. Beth never hid from a challenge. She wouldn't start now. She had very little left except her integrity.

"Gideon? Why are you back?" She couldn't help it if she didn't sound welcoming.

She knew she hadn't slept through the whole night.

"Something else has happened that you need to know about. Can we *cumme* in?"

We? "Who is with you?"

"It's Sergeant Beck, ma'am."

"*Ja. Cumme* in. And please, just call me Beth." Two sets of footsteps approached her bed. She shifted, fully aware of the thick bandages covering her eyes. Silently, she reprimanded herself for her vanity. Dropping her head back onto the pillow, she sighed. The beginning of a headache pulsed.

"You shouldn't move so fast," Gideon muttered. "You were hit on the head. Give yourself time to heal."

"*Ja, denke* Dr. Bender."

He chuckled. "Sorry. I didn't mean to get pushy."

The familiar cadence of a frequent argument between them eased some of her tension. Gideon was brighter than most people she knew. All right, he was brighter than everyone. And his brain held so many weird facts he'd learned.

What she missed most, though, were the practical jokes he'd play. Especially the ones he'd ask her to help him with.

Did he still do that, or had Miriam taken that part of him away, too?

She shook her head to displace the poorly timed mental meandering. He was standing in front of her, even if she couldn't see him.

"What can I help you with?"

A few seconds ticked by. She drummed her fingers on the bed while she waited for one of them to say something.

Finally, Sergeant Beck spoke up. "Beth, I'm sorry to inform you that a second body was discovered in your father's auction barn."

All the air left the room. She gasped, trying to breathe. "Wh—who was it?"

"We don't know. The person was burned beyond recognition. Beth, the person who died was murdered."

"What's happening?" she burst out suddenly. "People don't get killed at my *haus*. Why would anyone hurt someone like *Daed*?"

A tear leaked from her eye. The cotton gauze absorbed it. Great. Now the bandage over her right eye had a damp spot. She ignored it. She wanted answers. She wanted to mourn her father and pick up the pieces of her life and try to put them back together. Except there would forever be a hole there where her father would have stood. What was left for her? Would she continue to remain here in Ohio, where she'd grown up, or would she return to Pennsylvania and make her way with the distant relations they visited a few times a year?

"Beth." The edge of the bed sank a little as he settled his weight near her feet. "I know this is scary. We'll do all we can to help you."

She laughed, the sound harsh in the small room. "Gideon, what can you do to help?"

He might be smart, but he remained an Amish man who would never react with violence, not even to protect himself.

"What Steve didn't tell you was after the second body had been declared the victim of violence, his chief had him search your *haus* for any evidence that might lead us to why. Or who." He paused. Her heart thudded at the idea of them going through her home. "Every room had been torn apart."

She sucked in a breath, shocked to her core. "All of them?"

"Ja. In your room—"

He stopped. In her mind, she could picture him frowning, trying to piece together the easiest way to tell someone bad news.

"Rip off the Band-Aid, Gideon."

He sighed. "In your room, your dishes had been shattered. Like someone had taken a hammer to them. And your doll had been torn apart. Your room's been completely tossed."

She hadn't been familiar with that terminology previously, but she instantly envisioned the state of her room.

She gagged. Twisted away from them. A gentle hand cupped the back of her head. When she was through retching, embarrassment surged up. Her cheeks were on fire.

"Did I throw up on the floor?"

"Nee. I held a garbage can for you. It's *gut.*"

A foul taste lingered. "Ugh. I need to rinse my mouth."

"I can help you." Steve's voice responded. "I'm going into the bathroom. Be right back."

Hard shoe soles strode across the floor. A door creaked and a moment later she heard the water running. The water shut off and she listened to Steve's returning steps. He halted next to her.

"I have a cup of water and a bowl for you to rinse your mouth."

She did so, then settled back.

"They were starting to bring dinner around when we arrived, so we should get going. I have talked to the doctor. They'll move you to a private room this evening. Hospital security will watch the door," Steve told her.

That was fine for tonight. But where would she go tomorrow? This was so much worse than she had expected. The memory of her prior conversation with Gideon sprang to her mind.

"Gideon, is your offer still open? Can I stay with your family for a short time?" Hopefully, the police would find *Daed*'s killer immediately.

"*Ja*. You are *welkum* to *cumme* to my *haus*. And you can stay as long as you need."

It wasn't what she wanted, but she was out of options. She didn't want his pity, and she no longer trusted the bond of friendship they had once shared, but she needed help and a place to stay while the police investigated. His family had the benefit of being related to several branches of the law. Plus, she knew them well, even if they hadn't talked much for two years.

"I can't go home. *Ja,* I will stay with your family." Her mouth twisted. "It's the best choice at the moment, ain't so?"

"*Ja*. It's so."

Did he hear how she had emphasized his family? She wanted to make it clear that all was not well between them. It would have been easier if she could see his expression. Gideon had the most expressive blue eyes. It frustrated her not to see them now.

"*Gut*." The bed creaked and bounced a bit as he stood

up. "I will be here tomorrow morning to bring you home with me."

Before she could say more, she heard the door open and close. He didn't leave her time to change her mind. Despite herself, she huffed out a soft laugh. Gideon knew her well. She had changed her mind about decisions she'd made in the past.

Not this time, though. This time, she was stuck, unable to face the other alternative open to her. It wasn't like she had any other family nearby. They'd left the rest of their family behind in Spartansburg, Pennsylvania years ago. Her father had claimed there were too many bad memories in Pennsylvania. They needed a new location to start a new life.

Which meant she was practically a stranger to the rest of her relations. Her mind flashed back to the letter she'd received from Miriam. She couldn't remember if there was a return address or not. It would be typical of her sister to leave it off. It didn't matter. She had no way to respond to it without help, even if she were inclined to do so. For now, she'd keep the letter and its contents to herself.

Her roommate began to snore. She couldn't even converse with her. With the bandages covering her eyes, she had no sense of the time. It had been lunch time when she'd been attacked. She hadn't eaten anything since breakfast. Her stomach grumbled.

The door opened. "I hear someone needs a new room!" a soft male voice said.

Within ten minutes, she had been moved to a new room. The absence of her former roommate's noises and snoring made this space feel so empty.

The door opened again. "Dinner!"

Finally.

After a few moments of breezy conversation, the nurse directed her to where everything was on her tray. Potatoes at three o'clock. Green beans at six. Meat at ten. Jell-O sitting off to the right. Beth dug in to the potatoes and green beans, hoping she wasn't wearing any of them, then nibbled the meat. Yech. She'd move on to the orange gelatin. She splattered some on her cheek. When she went to wipe it off with her napkin, her hands bumped into the gauze covering her eyes. It felt damp. Frustrated, she tore off the offending bandages. Dropping them on the floor, she tried to finish her dinner. They'd have to replace the bandages in the morning. Sighing, she pushed the cart holding the tray aside.

Weariness pulled at her like an anchor dropped into the ocean. Settling back against the wafer thin excuse for a pillow, she allowed the gentle whirring of the hospital monitor to lull her into a light sleep. She woke when the door opened and footsteps approached the bed.

The nurse coming to remove her dinner tray, she assumed, waiting for the tray to be taken. The tray remained where it was, however. Queasy with unease, she tensed beneath the light blanket.

"Hello?"

She felt silly. She knew someone was there. Why wouldn't they speak? She waited.

"Are you here to take my tray? I'm done eating." Sweat beaded on her upper lip. Something was wrong, and she was helpless to do anything. If only she could see.

Instead of answering, a warm hand grabbed onto her arm, the fingers closing tightly around the limb.

"Ouch!"

Now she was wonderful scared. Before she could yell out, a sharp prick pierced her skin. She didn't know what was in the syringe, but she knew it wasn't for her health. She struggled against the iron grip but couldn't free herself.

"Wait! What are you doing?" Her words were slightly slurred. She'd wanted to shout her questions but had barely managed to mumble.

Within seconds, lethargy swept through her. The bed began to move. Her head flopped on the pillow. Her whole being called out for her to resist and fight against being pushed on the bed out of the room. She was helpless to obey. Within seconds, weightlessness washed over her, and the darkness pulled her under.

Would Gideon be able to find her? Before it was too late?

FIVE

Where was she?

Beth's arms tingled and ached. Why were they behind her? She tried to shift her position. The fog in her mind cleared. Her hands were tied! Her ankles were bound, too. She was lying on her side. It felt like she was still on the hospital bed.

The vibrations shivering through the metal meant the bed was in motion. She didn't hear any sound around her. Who was pushing the bed? Her vision remained dark, only shadows with light around the edges, giving her no information regarding her current location. Was she still in the hospital, or had she been taken outside?

Taking care to make no sound lest she draw attention to the fact that she was conscious, Beth squeezed her lids closed and tried to remember what had happened. She recalled the doctor in charge moving her to a private room. The sergeant had told him to do that. She ate dinner. Someone had entered her room. They'd squeezed her arm and sedated her. She recalled nothing after that until she had awakened a few moments earlier.

Why hadn't the person who had taken her killed her? If this was related to her father's death, and she couldn't imagine it being a coincidence, why was she still alive? She had no clues about her kidnapper's identity. He or she had strong fingers. She probably had bruises on her arm from where they held on to her. Her abductor hadn't said a single word. She inhaled through her nose, deep and slow. No obvious perfumes or other scents, such as a sporty deodorant. All she could smell was the antiseptic scent of a hospital.

And maybe…mildew?

Where would one find mildew in a hospital?

The bed hit a minor bump. The sound of the wheels smacking the ground echoed, as if they were in some kind of cavern. Gritting her teeth against the sudden pain, she held her groan in with an effort.

The basement. That was the only place she could think of. If there was a leak in a pipe or water damage, that would account for the mildew. But now what? She had no way to alert Gideon or anyone else about where she was.

Beth lay on the moving bed for what felt like an hour. She had no real reliable method to determine how much time had passed. The hospital cot continued moving at a smooth rate. Every once in a while, it would catch on something. Kind of like it was going over a crack in a sidewalk. Or as if the bed had traveled over an uneven or damaged spot on a concrete floor. By now, she was certain by the sound the wheels made that the ground was cement or concrete. Definitely not the linoleum that covered the halls in the rest of the hospital.

Finally, the bed came to a halt. Beth strained her ears, desperate to catch the smallest noise. Some clue to help her pinpoint her exact location. Her breathing hitched. Her heart hammered in her chest. If she didn't get her breathing under control, she'd hyperventilate. Even if she didn't, she'd alert her captor that she was awake. She didn't know why she was still alive, but she wanted to remain that way.

Sergeant Beck had told her he'd have a security guard by her room, watching over her. What had happened to the guard? Had he become another victim? None of this was her fault, but she had no desire for anyone to suffer in her place or because of her.

Shuffling footsteps approached and stopped next to her head. She held herself still. In her head, she repeated the words, "Help me." *Gott* would understand.

The person standing over her bent down. She felt their breath on her cheek. It brought the strong odor of garlic and onion with it. Instinctively, she cringed back, her eyes flying open.

"So, I was right. You were faking," an amused voice said. It was a male voice. And a voice she had never heard before.

"What do you want with me?" There was no point in pretending anymore. Her voice trembled.

"I don't want anything with you. I'm just getting paid to leave you here." The lack of emotion in the statement chilled her. She quaked from the inside out.

Whoever he was, he sounded young. Too young to be a killer.

"Please. They'll kill me. You have to help me escape."

"Sorry. No can do. I always keep my promises."

He stopped talking. Hard-soled shoes clomped on the floor toward them. "And so do I."

The voice was older, rougher, reminding her of sandpaper.

"I've delivered her, sir. Just like I said." The younger voice came faster, higher. He was nervous. Whoever had entered the room terrified him.

"So I see." The cold voice reeked of distain.

A pause. "My payment? I did what you asked."

"Ah, yes. I did promise to pay you. Here it is." Now amusement rang in the other man's tones. Malicious amusement.

Another pause.

"No—"

Crack!

The gunshot echoed in the room. Beth recoiled. The next noise she heard sounded like something being dragged across the floor. He'd killed the young man without any hesitation. She had no doubt she was facing her father's killer. She could envision the beard. The anger emanating from him.

If she escaped this impossible situation, she'd see that face for the rest of her life.

"What are you staring at?"

She nearly laughed at the irony in the question. "Nothing. I can't see anything."

A movement near her face. Tendrils of hair lifted from her forehead. Was he fanning his hand before her eyes?

"Well, maybe you can't see now. But you could see inside your house before. Where did he hide it?"

"I don't understand what you're talking about."

"You better figure it out fast. The only reason you're still alive is because I need to know where the stash is. Where did he hide it?"

"What stash? And who hid it? My father? I don't know what you mean." Panic clawed at her throat.

The man scoffed. "Are you playing me?"

She shook her head, desperately wishing she could see. She'd never been so vulnerable in her life.

"Please. I don't understand."

"Drugs. Where did your dear old dad hide the drugs?"

She gasped, shocked to her soul. Then she vehemently shook her head. "*Nee*. You're wrong. He would never become involved in drug trafficking."

She didn't care what he said. Her father had been a *gut* and honest man. She'd never believe otherwise.

Gideon had said someone had been inside her *haus*. Now she knew who. And she knew why. Sort of.

"We'll see what you remember after sitting here awhile in the cold. Maybe you'll feel more cooperative. If you don't freeze to death first."

The bed was wheeled a short distance. The distinct clang of a door shutting and locking sent chills through her blood. She couldn't sit here, waiting to die.

Struggling, she wiggled around, trying to sit up. It was difficult without the use of her hands. The cot swayed with her movements. The wheels squeaked in protest. Twisting, she rotated too far and suddenly fell off the side of the cot, landing on her left side, the breath knocked out of her.

The temperature of the icy floor seeped through her gown. She was out of ideas.

Resting her forehead against the smooth, cool surface, she let the tears flow.

Gideon wandered out onto the back porch after dinner. Although he loved his family dearly, the chatter and clank of dishes was too much for him to handle. His conscience silently berated him, regardless of the fact that he had done nothing wrong. It didn't help to remind himself of that.

He had left Beth in the hospital, alone and lost.

Despite the clear vibes she'd given that she had no desire to be in his presence, he still believed he should have stayed. Maybe not in the room where she was trying to sleep. But in the general vicinity so he'd be near if she needed him.

Which was ridiculous. Why would she suddenly decide, after not having him around in over eight hundred days of their lives, that she couldn't do without his assistance? In the Amish world, neighbors were always willing to lend a hand. She'd be inundated with people providing her with food. Clothes. Shelter. Everything she could want.

Except her family.

He thought back to the moment he and Steve had entered the *haus* two hours before.

Steve's face had lit up the second he'd spotted Joss's car in her parents' driveway. Gideon had teased him half-heartedly, but it had warmed his heart. Joss herself had been waiting at the back door when he and Steve returned from the hospital. She kissed her husband the moment he walked up the steps onto the back porch. Although his parents were affectionate people, they didn't care for public displays such as kissing. Gideon's brothers all tried to avoid kissing their spouses in front of *Mamm* and *Daed*. But not his sister. Gideon was happy for her, but the niggle of envy stirring in his gut unsettled him. He would never begrudge her the joy she'd found. He only wished for some chance for similar happiness in his future.

Strangely, Miriam's face wasn't the one in his head at the moment. It was Beth. He shook his head. He'd never thought of Beth as anything but a friend before.

"Steve, you'll stay for dinner, *ja*?" Edith beamed and greeted her son-in-law when he took off his hat and hung it on the hook inside the door. Gideon's mother took great pleasure in feeding and caring for her expanding family.

"I'd never turn down your cooking, Edith. Absolutely. Are the kids around here somewhere?"

Gideon had stopped paying attention to the conversation. Beth's pale face swam before him. Her *daed* had died and she was alone. He tried to be his normal self over dinner. But somehow his jokes and teasing had felt flat. Judging from the glances he got from his parents, Joss and Steve, his family noted his distracted mood. True to their nature, though, they didn't comment, but allowed him his privacy. That would only last for so long.

The door opened behind him. He recognized Joss's light steps immediately and smiled. He'd known she'd be the first one to seek him out. How had he managed twenty-two years without his twin sister in his life? He thanked *Gott* every day that she'd returned to them.

"You want to tell me about it?" Joss settled herself on the top stair next to him. She rested her forearms on her knees and folded her hands as if she had all the time in the world.

Did he want to speak about it? He had half decided he didn't but surprised himself by opening his mouth and pouring out the horror of the day to her.

"Poor Beth," she commiserated. "That's a lot. Losing your only parent like that."

With a shock, he realized she'd gone through something similar. Although the woman who raised her hadn't been her mother, she'd always thought she was. She'd been taken from Joss abruptly. Violently. Slinging an arm around his sister's shoulder, he hugged her close for a few seconds, then released her. They sat in silence for a full minute.

Joss shifted to peer at him. "I haven't heard you talk of her in a long time. Or any of the family. You used to mention them all the time."

"*Ja*. It's been a few years."

She didn't press. But the dam had been opened. He told her about his friendship with Beth. And about falling in love with Miriam. By the time he'd mentioned how Miriam had led him to believe she'd be open to a proposal days before running off with another, he couldn't stop talking. It all came out. Even the way he'd distanced himself from the family. And the guilt and confusion boiling up inside now.

"Hmm."

He glanced at his sister. The hard, angry look on her normally kind face sent shock spiraling in his head.

"Joss?"

"I met Miriam a time or two. Not enough to know her, but she would not have made you a good wife. Bone selfish, that one. She seemed like one of those girls who liked having all the adoration. You are better off without her influence. As for Beth, she's as steady as they come. Give her time. You two were friends for most of your life. What you did was wrong—" he winced "—but don't give up on her. She may forgive you."

Inside, Steve's phone rang, making a sound like a barking dog. He and Joss shared a smile. It always amused them. No doubt his *mamm* jumped at the intrusive ringtone. The first time it had happened, she'd gasped, looking around for the dog. In the Amish world, dogs did not belong in a *haus*. When Steve had bought Joss a puppy and they let Max have the run of their *haus,* his parents had bitten their tongues and not interfered. But he knew it hadn't been easy.

The smiles slid from their faces when Steve burst out the door. "Gideon. Joss. I need to go. The security guard at the hospital was found knocked out. Beth is missing."

"I'll see you at home," Joss said, leaping to her feet. "You can text me if you run into any trouble."

Gideon didn't say a word. He dashed away from the stairs and ducked into the passenger side of the cruiser. Steve didn't argue as he slid behind the wheel, though he did send Gideon a quick glance. When a person went missing, extra eyes on the ground were never refused.

Gideon buckled his seat belt and started praying. He should never have left her.

The cruiser turned onto the road and Steve pressed down

on the accelerator. "She can't have been taken far. The hospital was on alert. It would have been difficult to get her past all the security. They have someone going over the footage at the exits now. And she was in her new room when dinner was served. So, our timeline is—she disappeared within the last hour and a half."

Too much time. Gideon crushed his lips together to keep the words inside. A lot could happen in ninety minutes. For a person willing to burn an entire barn down to murder one person and then kill an innocent man to hide that death, killing one woman who might have seen him wasn't that much of a stretch.

He needed to do something. Anything. Pounding his fist against his knee, Gideon scanned the horizon as the police cruiser sped past. When the vehicle stopped at a stop sign and waited for a slow moving garbage truck to rumble through the intersection, he was ready to crawl out of his own skin. Still, he kept his impatient thoughts to himself.

The intersection was clear. Steve stomped on the gas. Reaching out, he switched on the sirens and the flashing lights. Gideon grabbed the handle at the top of the door. He completely agreed when Steve increased velocity, but his stomach dipped as they hit a pothole and the vehicle bounced. Ahead of them, the traffic parted, cars and pickup trucks all moving to the side of the road to let the police cruiser pass.

They made it to the hospital in record time. But was it quick enough?

The hospital doors were locked. Impatiently, they waited to be cleared and buzzed in. Once inside, the two men raced inside the building. Gideon crashed into the reception desk, his hands out in front of him to brace himself for the impact. The woman behind the desk jumped back, knocking her headset askew.

The hospital security chief was at their side instantly, rattling off what had been done to locate Beth since her absence had been discovered. "All entrances have been locked. The rooms are still being searched, but so far, no signs of her have been seen. One of our maintenance crew is missing."

"That's a possible link. Search your video for him, as well as her."

"We're still viewing it."

His radio crackled to life. The chief hit the button. "What do you have?"

"Sir! Joel was seen on the video pushing a hospital bed into the basement elevator."

"Out of my way!" The burly security man charged toward the exit, with Steve and Gideon on his heels. They slammed through the heavy door and pounded down the metal steps, making no effort to be silent. The heels of their shoes rang out like cymbals crashing together. The temperature dropped with each foot closer to the basement floor.

"Joel!"

Gideon nearly smacked into the security chief's back. The man knelt on one knee next to a young man lying half under the stairs. Steve flashed his light on the missing maintenance worker. Death had come quick, forever stamping an expression of horror on his face. He couldn't have been more than eighteen or nineteen. Too young. Gideon's stomach clenched. Was Beth dead?

Nee. It did no *gut* to go there. They needed to continue searching.

He moved ahead of them, ignoring Steve's voice calling his name. He had to locate Beth. Urgency flooded him. He scanned the room, narrowing his gaze to see better in the shadows.

A sudden noise made him stop to listen.

That was a scream.

Beth!

Bursting into a run, he pelted toward the scream, aware of the other men rushing behind him. He twisted around a corner. A half-open door was thirty feet ahead. Twenty. He crashed into the room without slowing. The door swung open the rest of the way, whacking a man off his feet. A gun skittered to the floor. It slowed and landed next to Beth.

She was bound on the cold cement, her face and arms bruised.

Gideon ignored the man on the floor and rushed to her side. Gently, he searched for additional injuries. She was conscious, but he didn't like the blue tinge around her lips. He shed his jacket and started to wrap her up in it.

She needed to be cut free before she could put her arms through the sleeves.

"Steve! I need your pocketknife."

"Hold him," Steve ordered the security guard. Kneeling beside Gideon and Beth, Steve pulled out his knife and sawed through the bindings at her ankles, then at her wrists.

Beth cried out.

"I know," Gideon soothed. "It hurts when the blood starts circulating freely again. Beth, I need to get you warm."

Moving as gently as possible, hating that he was hurting her, he worked the coat over her arms. She bit her lip, her face scrunched in pain. Her limbs had been forcibly held in that position for up to two hours. The agony must be intense.

He couldn't help it. The cold was the real threat. And shock.

He hoisted the shivering woman in his arms and stood.

The man in the security guard's hold glared at him. He recalled the description Beth had given of the man who'd shot her dad. The lack of a black beard was minor. These days, anyone could alter their appearance through chemical dyes or shaving. And the hazel eyes didn't matter either. Beth had declared she hadn't seen their color because the killer had been wearing sunglasses.

Amos had been the same height as Gideon. Five foot ten. Beth had described the man who attacked her as being two or three inches taller than her father. Visually measuring this man, Gideon placed him at five foot eight.

"This isn't the man who killed Amos."

SIX

Beth jolted upright in Gideon's arms at his words. She moved so quick, the top of her head clipped his chin.

"Sorry!" she muttered before focusing on what he'd said. "You're sure that he's not the one? How can you be sure? I wasn't able to give you that much description. Not enough for a sketch." Not that she doubted him. Gideon's ability to sort through facts and reach the correct conclusion was nearly always on point.

It was relationships he apparently struggled with. She pushed that aside. Now wasn't the time to relive the past.

"You told us enough. The man who shot your *daed* was several inches taller. Say at least six foot tall. This man is only five foot eight."

Neither she nor Steve questioned the accuracy of the height he'd spouted out so casually. They had both seen him at work before. With his words, however, all hope that the danger had passed disintegrated into dust.

"We can discuss this in a few minutes," Steve interrupted. "I need to get this guy booked. And Beth needs to be checked out by a doctor—"

"I'm not staying another day in this hospital." Beth had been raised to never interrupt an authority figure, but she'd had enough. They obviously couldn't protect her here. She had never been comfortable in such sterile surroundings. After today, if she never entered another hospital, that would be fine with her. A shiver started at her head and worked its way down. She tightened her jaw to stave off the shuddering, but her teeth continued to chatter.

"You're freezing!" Gideon's arms tightened around her. "Let's get you someplace warm."

She should protest. Tell him she was capable of walking. But the truth was, she didn't know if she could stand. The torturous sensation of pins and needles dancing along her arms and legs had faded, but they ached like she was going on eighty-eight instead of twenty-eight.

Sighing, she allowed her head to droop onto his shoulder. She'd never been in his arms before. It was a warm, cozy place to be. She hadn't felt safe since before she'd rushed into the yard—how long ago had it been?

"What time is it?" she murmured.

"Going on nine in the evening," Gideon responded, his breath fanning across her forehead. She flushed. "I was planning on picking you up in the morning around ten."

"I'm not staying here tonight." That was nonnegotiable.

"Nee, you're not," he agreed. "We have a room for you to stay in. Tomorrow, we'll go back to your *haus* and collect some clothes, once Steve gives us the go-ahead. But you'll be staying at my place. My *mamm* will insist. You can't make me disappoint my *mamm*, ain't so?"

As chilled and exhausted as she was, she grinned tiredly at the teasing words. Edith Bender was well-known for her hospitality. Being spoiled for a bit by his *mamm* would be *welkum,* indeed.

She nearly dozed off in his arms as he carried her up the stairs. A sudden memory intruded before she succumbed to sleep. Pushing her head off his shoulder, she frowned, pulling the memory into focus.

"What's wrong?" Gideon asked before she could speak.

"There was another man. He drugged me and took me to the basement." Was it her imagination or had Gideon growled? She couldn't have heard that right. "I heard them arguing. The first man had promised to bring me to him." She gestured vaguely behind her. "When he asked about getting paid, the man you found with me today shot him. I heard him drag him away." She couldn't make herself say she thought he'd died.

A long silence followed her words. Her stomach clenched and she pressed a hand against it to ease the sensation.

"He's dead, ain't so?"

"*Ja*. We found his body before we heard you scream."

"What was his name?" Her throat ached.

"Joel."

Wincing, she turned her face back into his shoulder. Tears stung the back of her eyes. The young man hadn't hesitated to bring her to her own death for money. He had done evil to her. He'd drugged her and tied her hands and feet. All for greed.

But no life should be taken lightly. She was not his judge.

"Beth? Are you alright?" She didn't require sight to catch the hint of worry coloring Gideon's tone.

"*Ja*. I'm *gut*. Or I will be. It's sad though, ain't so? He sounded so young. And now he's dead."

"He was young." Steve's voice came from the right. "But he made some very bad choices. I agree—it's sad. But choices have consequences. It would have been sadder had you been seriously hurt."

Gideon grunted, a sound that could have been agreement.

Sighing, she rested for a few moments, letting the men

take charge for a bit. Steve and the security chief arranged for a Sutter Springs officer to drive over and take charge of the criminal. Steve wanted to review the rest of the footage and see if he could find when and how Joel's killer had entered the establishment. If he'd gotten in after the lockdown, then someone inside had to have assisted him.

When asked, she told them Joel had not left her side once she awoke, but she couldn't tell them about anything while she was sedated. She'd been out for over an hour. Gideon borrowed Steve's phone and called his brother Isaiah to give him and Beth a ride back to his parents' *haus*.

"Joss would have been closer, but she has the kids. Plus, I don't want to put her at risk. Isaiah and Micah are both skilled at handling these situations," Gideon told Beth.

Right. Because Micah was a deputy US Marshal and Isaiah had been a bounty hunter who now worked in security systems. She hated that she was the reason any of his family would be in a dangerous situation. However, if he had to call someone, Isaiah or Micah would be the best options.

"I didn't know they lived so close."

"Micah is about an hour away. Isaiah and Addie, his wife, recently found a *haus* in Sutter Springs. He wanted to be closer to my parents."

It made sense. Isaiah had left home when he was seventeen. Since reconnecting with his family, she understood why he'd want to be close by. He'd already missed so much.

Sooner than she would have liked, Beth was being poked and prodded by the doctor again. As she suspected, she had sustained multiple bruises, but no real damage. At least not physically. Emotionally, she didn't know how she'd sleep peacefully ever again. What the doctor was really concerned about was the possibility that she had suffered a concussion when she had fallen off the cot and her head had collided with the cement floor.

"You've already suffered enough head trauma today. The last thing you need is another injury. I don't know how this will affect your vision returning," the doctor had said.

Prod, prod. Poke. She ignored it while his words whirled around inside her head. Any complaints she had about the extensive reexamination died in her throat. What if her vision loss was permanent? How would she care for herself while she learned to cope without that sense? Her blood changed to ice in her veins.

She didn't want to return to Pennsylvania. She and *daed* had visited those relatives every year, but she didn't want to live with them. She had made a life in Sutter Springs. She wanted to stay where she was. Just not in the same *haus*.

It was almost eleven by the time the doctor declared she didn't have a concussion. Exhausted, she held on to Gideon's arm and walked out of the hospital to where his brother was waiting. Gideon tucked her into the back seat of Isaiah's car, then seated himself in the front passenger seat. Weariness swamped her and she slumped against the door, her head resting against the window. Her *kapp* absorbed the coolness from the glass. Sighing, she closed her eyes. The vibrations of the vehicle coaxed her into a light doze.

Until the rear wheel hit a bump.

"Ouch." She lifted her head away from the window.

"Oops. Sorry, didn't see that one," Isaiah apologized.

"Not a problem."

"Denke for picking us up, Isaiah," Gideon's voice said from the front seat. "I appreciate the ride. I hope Addie wasn't upset."

Guilt poked at her. She bit her lip.

Isaiah scoffed. "Don't worry about it. You know my wife

adores you. If I hadn't wanted to help, she and Ollie would have convinced me."

Gideon chuckled. "Ollie is a *gut* boy."

"Yeah, he is. Addie told me her only worry is he likes to emulate his uncle Gideon's practical jokes too much."

"I've been *gut,* lately. I haven't done anything for her to complain about."

"Much."

They laughed again.

"How is she feeling?"

"Oh, fine. Pregnancy agrees with her. Only three months to go, then our little girl will make her debut. Ollie can't wait to meet his baby sister."

Listening from the back seat, Beth flushed. She'd never heard men speak so openly of pregnancy! At the same time, it touched her—the love saturating Isaiah's deep tones every time he spoke of his wife or *kinder.* Would she ever hear such from a husband?

She bowed her head to hide her face, just in case they were watching. She already knew the answer. At twenty-seven, her chances of finding a husband were very slim. All of her friends had married before they turned twenty-one.

Then she mentally shook herself. Why waste time on thinking of love or marriage? She needed to worry about surviving. Maybe after the man who had murdered her father and was out to kill her was caught, she could revisit the idea of finding a husband.

If the killer didn't find her first.

The clock on Isaiah's dashboard flipped to eleven thirty-two as they rolled into the driveway. Isaiah parked the car next to the back porch and shut off the engine. Gideon glanced into the kitchen window, his view unfettered by curtains like he saw in the windows of non-Amish homes. The Amish didn't care for such *frippery*, as his *mamm* called them, and considered curtains to be decorative and unnecessary. He and his *daed* had made green blinds and hung them on the front room and bedroom windows. Inside the kitchen, a soft light glowed. Which meant at least one of his parents was still awake. They had several propane lamps hanging on the walls in each room. The light appeared lower. His parents must have pushed the mobile unit with the large propane tank on it into the kitchen.

Letting himself out of the vehicle, he gently shut the door in an attempt to keep the noise down.

He opened Beth's door, expecting to find her asleep, and saw her chocolate brown gaze staring sightlessly ahead.

"Hey. We're here. At my *haus*." He grimaced. Where else would they be.

She nodded. Taking her elbow, he led her to the stairs. "You're at the base of the steps. There are four of them. The steps are all seven and a half inches tall, and eleven inches deep."

"Ja." Reaching out with her free arm, she grabbed hold of the railing and climbed with outward confidence. An outsider wouldn't have guessed she was nervous. Gideon felt the hesitation because he still had hold of her elbow.

They arrived at the back door as his *mamm* opened it wide. He expected her to move out of the way and allow them to pass by. Instead, she moved forward and took Beth in her embrace, murmuring soft words in the younger woman's ear. Her hand moving in soothing circles on Beth's back.

Beth had been strong all day. At Edith Bender's touch, she folded like her bones had dissolved, her head sinking onto the other woman's shoulder, and wept. Gideon stiffened his jaw as her grief hit him, his own eyes stinging. Isaiah clapped a hand on his shoulder.

"Steady," his older brother cautioned. "I'll be off so you can get her settled. I'll come out tomorrow. Use the phone in the shop if you need anything. Don't worry about the time."

"I won't." Gideon waved as Isaiah drove off. *Mamm* anchored an arm around Beth's waist and ushered her into the *haus*. Beyond them, *Daed* stood in the middle of the kitchen, waiting for them.

Gideon stood frozen, staring at Beth at his mother's side. In his mind, she'd always been sturdy. He and Beth had climbed trees together and raced each other on fair weather days. She was only a few inches shorter than him, and he'd seen her haul hay and milk cows with the practiced ease of one used to hard labor. Once, she'd even assisted Zeke shoeing a lame mare. Beth was a hardy soul.

In that instant, his view of her shifted. He noted how slim her waist was. *Mamm*'s arm was able to reach all the way around. Her weeping had awoken his protective instincts in a way he'd never experienced. He dropped his eyes, embarrassed to be thinking of his *gut* friend in that way. They were barely mending their relationship. He didn't want to risk it by bringing in other factors. Attraction meant nothing if it killed any chance of winning her respect back.

Plus, what woman would want her sister's leavings?

Gott, help me forgive Miriam for all the damage she wrought in my life. In our lives.

He didn't feel an immediate sense of peace and forgiveness, but he hadn't expected to. In his experience, *Gott* worked at His own pace. Gideon would have to be consistent in his prayer and repentance. It didn't matter. Faith was a way of life. *Gott* was the center of it all. He'd do what he needed to do to keep right with *Gott*.

Realizing his parents had left the kitchen and moved into the family room, his *daed* pushing the mobile propane lamp ahead of him, Gideon strode into the *haus*. He kicked off his boots and left them on the mat by the door then plucked his hat off his head. Placing it on the hook next to his father's hat, he ran a hand through his hair. The glow of the light stopped. They'd reached the front room. Clasping his hands behind his back, Gideon followed behind.

Mamm fussed over Beth for five minutes until the younger woman yawned.

"Cumme," his *mamm* announced. "I will put you in the room down the hall, here on the first floor."

Gut. She wouldn't have to climb steps in the middle of the night. Gideon spoke with his father quietly, telling him everything that had occurred that horrible day. *Daed* would relay it all to his mother. When his mother reappeared fifteen minutes later, Gideon said good night and sought refuge in his own room. He needed his space to think through everything that he'd seen, heard and felt that day.

At the end of the day, Gideon liked to take some time for himself. Joss said he needed to "decompress." He always laughed at the term.

"I'm not a balloon," he told her.

But the term wasn't that inaccurate. Days like now, he felt like there was too much pressure inside and he needed time to release some of it. Moving to the window, he stared outside, marveling like always at the constellations and the immensity of *Gott*'s creation. The night sky fascinated him.

A yawn caught him off guard. Glancing up, he saw the clouds moving in, blocking the stars from view. Tomorrow would be a rainy day.

Changing into his pajamas, he went to bed. He was tired, but his mind refused to wind down. He rolled over. It was going to be a long night.

The gentle rumble of distant thunder woke him.

Opening his eyes, he knew it was much too early to rise. Yanking his thin blanket over his shoulders, he closed his eyes, determined to sleep another hour.

Five minutes later, he tossed the covers aside and stood. He wouldn't be able to sleep, not with the way his mind was racing. He needed action to work off some of his energy. Dressing quickly, he headed to the kitchen and made coffee. When it was done, he grabbed a mug and made his way out to the barn. He might as well get a head start on some of the morning chores. The glow of the sunrise filtered through the clouds.

He milked the cows and took care of the horses and chickens. *Daed* joined him as he was finishing.

"Well, *sohn*, did you leave any work for me?"

"Not much. I had trouble sleeping, so I figured I'd get started. Later this morning, I want to bring Beth to her *haus* to pack her things. Will that be *gut*?"

"Absolutely. I am sorry about Amos."

Gideon was, too. He excused himself to call Steve and check on the status of the *haus*. Fortunately, Steve had expected his call and had already been in touch with the crime scene lab. After thanking his brother-in-law, he hung up and strode back to where his father was straightening up the tools in the front of the shop.

"Your *mamm* should have breakfast ready."

Together, they trudged back to the *haus*. Edith and Beth were both in the kitchen, though judging by the dark smudges under her brown eyes, Beth hadn't gotten any more sleep than he did. The chocolate brown irises were surrounded by bloodshot whites. She'd been crying in her room. Who wouldn't?

He sat at the table next to her. "I called Steve from the shop about fifteen minutes ago." She nodded around a mouthful of eggs. "He said…"

He hated to refer to her *haus* as a crime scene. It sounded so cold and insensitive.

She took a deep swallow of water and wiped her mouth with a cloth napkin. "Just say it, Gideon. I know you're not trying to hurt my feelings. But seriously, I don't think my heart could hurt more than it does now."

Briefly, he covered her hand with his. Recalling the way she'd shaken him off the day before, he didn't allow the touch to linger. Dropping his hand back to the table, he continued speaking. "He said the crime scene workers have been through the *haus* and gathered all the evidence they could. They have taken pictures of everything. We are not to do anything more than gather what you need—and no more, to be on the safe side."

"We should get it over with sooner rather than later, right? I want to be done with it."

He agreed and started to lean in. He caught himself, appalled at his behavior. What was he thinking? He'd nearly kissed her cheek. Beth and he had known each other for most of their lives, and he had never once kissed her cheek. Never been tempted to do so.

Until today.

SEVEN

A few moments later, Beth heard Gideon set his fork and knife on his plate. Was he done already? His chair legs scraped against the floor as he pushed away from the table. He stood and muttered something about hooking up the mare to the buggy, then left before she could respond. She sighed. She'd been so blunt. She'd probably appeared a bit nasty and bitter. That wasn't her. She tended to be upbeat and more optimistic.

Or she had been once. Had the past few years made her bitter?

She took a sip of her water. It was tepid, but she drank it anyway.

At the age of fifteen, Beth had learned about her sister's selfish side. Their friend Susannah had gone to her very first singing. Beth couldn't wait to hear about it. Back then, listening to Miriam talk about the singings seemed so thrilling. To be able to sit across from the boys, knowing one of them might ask for the privilege of driving you home. And one day that would lead to walking out with a young man, and from their marriage and a family of her own.

She and Susannah had giggled for days, dreaming about how wonderful the singing would be.

The Monday after the singing, Susannah refused to walk

to the local quilt shop with Beth. They'd always walked there together every Monday. Both of them were avid quilters, and it gave them a chance to talk and laugh while enjoying the outdoors.

But Susannah wouldn't go. Later, Beth learned Susannah had gone with another girl, one they'd liked well enough but hadn't been particular friends with. Crushed, she had tried to recall what she had done wrong.

It had never occurred to her to ask Miriam what *she* had done. She'd finally gone to Susannah and demanded she talk with her. She stood on Susannah's porch and told her she wasn't leaving until she knew what she had done to destroy their friendship.

Susannah admitted that it hadn't been Beth. She had sat across from Caleb Schultz at the singing. She knew he'd ask her if he could drive her home. Beth knew Susannah liked Caleb more than any boys. The evening had gone well. Until Miriam had decided she wanted Caleb to take *her* home. She'd flirted and cajoled him. When he left with Miriam, she'd glanced back over her shoulder at Susannah and given her what could only be called a wicked sneer. That's when she knew it had been done on purpose.

Beth had learned the lesson. She had never let on who she preferred. And life had been fine. Until she turned twenty and Miriam somehow figured it out.

Nope. She refused to dwell on it. Suddenly she realized Gideon was waiting for her outside. With Edith's help, she made it outside and down to the buggy.

"*Ack*. I would have *cumme* for you, Beth." Gideon placed a warm arm on her elbow and led her to the buggy. "The step is right in front of you. Do you need to know how far off the ground?"

Laughing, she shook her head. "*Nee*. I've been in enough

buggies to know. Even if I can't recall, my leg knows how high."

"Muscle memory," he replied.

"Only you would know there was a name for it." She lifted her leg the exact height and stepped up, his arm supporting her.

"Oh. Sorry?"

"It's not a bad thing, Gideon. You know I always enjoyed hearing you talk about facts no one else knew." It was true. His random knowledge had never seemed odd to her. She enjoyed the opportunity to learn new ideas from him.

The vehicle swayed with his weight when he climbed up beside her. She heard him take a deep breath, and then flick the reins, giving the horse the command to walk. At the street, he moved the beast onto the road and coaxed her to a trot. The air smelled of spring. Wet earth, flowers, the aroma of farm animals drifting over the fields.

"How's the vision this morning?"

She blinked. "I think it's a little brighter. Not so shadowy. I can see edges more clearly."

"I'm sorry. You know that, right?"

She blinked up at him, wishing she could see more than the outline of his shape. "For avoiding me?"

"*Ja.* That. And more. I don't want to hurt you, but I think your sister…"

He paused. That was Gideon. Starting to say something, then thinking how rude it might have sounded later. "Just say it, Gideon."

How often did she tell him that? She bit back a smile so he wouldn't think she was laughing at him.

"Well, I never really thought about your sister growing up. She was always your sister. And then suddenly, one day, she was there. I never thought about it, but the last time I

talked with her, she laughed at me. She said she never intended to marry me. I was too bookish for her. She only
wanted to have some fun. She also said it was *gut* for me
to be seen with someone other than you."

Beth sucked in a breath, stunned. She had known her
sister had targeted him because of their friendship. Instinct
and experience had told her that. But for him to confirm it?
Oh, it hurt.

Her sister was not a nice person. What was she going to
do about it? The knowledge of Miriam's unanswered letter
burned in her soul.

"She wants to *cumme* home," Beth blurted. Immediately,
she wished she could call the words back.

Gideon didn't say anything for a long time. Her shoulders
grew tighter with each passing second.

Finally, he cleared his throat. "I'm not sure what to say.
I know she's your sister. I remember being ecstatic when
Joss returned. But I have to be honest. I might eventually
forgive Miriam for the hurt she has caused both of us. But
I will never again trust her."

She so wanted to believe him. For the moment, she let
the subject drop.

Silence settled between them. Beth pondered his words.

"We're here."

Straightening in her seat, Beth clasped her hands together and held them tightly against her stomach, fighting
the sudden queasiness that had taken hold. This would be
one of the hardest things she ever set out to do. The funeral
would be harder.

"Wait there, Beth. I'll *cumme* and help you down." The
buggy tipped slightly when he disembarked. His footsteps
pounded in the dirt. He jogged around to reach her. All the

confidence of the morning dissipated. "Here I am. Grab on to my hand."

She caught his hand and clenched her fingers around it. Gideon didn't complain about her grip. Her fingers ached, but she couldn't seem to loosen them up.

Her feet touched the ground. The outline of the *haus* loomed up ahead. No individual details of the place stood out. Her memory made up for it. She visualized the picture window in front, the open porch, the white paint and the familiar step leading to the back door.

"Are you ready?" Gideon's breath brushed the curls at the side of her face. She shivered. "It's okay if you can't do this."

She straightened her shoulders and forced herself to ease her grip. The bearded man had taken what was left of her family. She would not allow him to destroy her courage or have any more of her life. "*Nee*. We need to do this. Let's go."

With Gideon's assistance, she made it into the back door of the *haus*. She entered and started to walk across the familiar wooden floor.

"Hold on." Gideon kicked something out of the way.

Her stomach dropped. She'd almost forgotten. "It's a mess, ain't so?"

"*Ja*. I'm sorry, Beth. But there is stuff everywhere."

She blinked the hot tears back. "It's only material things. Sergeant Beck said not to disturb anything else."

"Steve."

"Huh?"

"He's my brother-in-law. Call him Steve."

She shrugged. "Upstairs?"

"Do you want me to describe anything?"

She shuddered. "*Nee!* I don't want to know any more than I absolutely have to know. Let's go to my room so I can pack my bag and go."

Steadily, they climbed the thirteen steps that led upstairs. The second floor had three bedrooms and a bathroom. Their family in Pennsylvania did not have inside plumbing. However, in Sutter Springs, most of the homes did have simple bathrooms. The doors to the bedrooms immediately on either side of the landing started above the last stair. When they opened the bedrooms, she'd gotten used to the fact that the back third of the door did not line up with the landing and one needed to step through the last two thirds, or else risk falling down the stairwell.

"This landing isn't lined up with the door," Gideon said, almost as if it offended him.

She laughed. "I know that."

It was the last time she laughed while inside the *haus*. Gideon hadn't been exaggerating about the level of destruction. The moment she set foot inside her room, shards of china crunched under her boots. Her breath stalled in her lungs.

When she opened her mouth to speak, it came out as a soft whimper. Immediately, Gideon was at her side, holding her hand in his. She leaned into him, taking strength from his presence.

"Is your suitcase in your closet?"

She nodded. "*Ja*. It's purple."

He gave a weak chuckle. "Why doesn't that surprise me?"

She liked purple. Avoiding thinking of the pretty lavender flowers broken beneath the heel of her boot, she crossed to the dresser. "Put the suitcase on the dresser. Grab two or three dresses. I don't care which ones."

"I can do that." She heard him rustling around inside the closet. "If you want, I can step out and you can put on a fresh dress."

"That would be wonderful." She waited until he handed her the dress.

"It's the light purple one."

She nodded. It didn't matter what color it was. She couldn't see it anyway.

When he left the room, closing the door behind him, she did what she could and changed quickly. Once that was done, she found her stock of prayer *kapps*. She kept them on the table beside her bed. Swiftly, she brushed her hair and pinned it up in a bun. Then she held the hair in place with one hand and fumbled in the drawer for her bobby pins. Once the bun was secure, she gathered a *kapp* and secured it on her head. It was amazing how much better it felt to have a fresh *kapp* on her head.

While he was out of the room, she gathered the other necessities and put them on the bed. She would put them into the suitcase when he returned.

He knocked.

"I'm ready." When he entered the room and had shut the door behind himself again, she smiled in his direction. "*Denk*e. Did you get the other dresses and the suitcase?"

"Doing that now. Here's the suitcase. Whoa… What is this?"

"What is what?"

She couldn't imagine what he would find so interesting about a closet.

Gideon removed the dark plum colored suitcase from the top shelf of the attic and carefully tossed it onto the bed. He didn't want to disturb anything, but curiosity burned inside of him. He pushed at the loose panel at the top of her closet. As he'd suspected it would, it lifted. Shifting it to the side, he saw what appeared to be the entrance to an attic.

Did Beth know it was there?

He needed a ladder or a chair. Some way to get high enough to peer into the attic. He also needed a light so he could see what was up there. The *haus* had electricity installed at one time but not anymore. The rules of their *Ordnung* demanded that within a year of purchasing an *Englisch* home, it must be painted white, and all electricity needed to be stripped out of it. At one time, the rules insisted that the plumbing needed to be removed as well. Some Old Order districts continued to insist upon that.

Sutter Springs had elected to allow indoor plumbing. However, the lighting and heat systems could not be electric. The only place bathrooms were not allowed were in the schools. The Amish schools continued to use outdoor bath closets for students.

Backing away from the closet, he glanced around.

Beth waited patiently near the suitcase, arms crossed. She'd already packed some things from her dresser. He spied a couple of clean *kapps* lying on top. It looked like some things hadn't been trashed.

Wait. She'd asked him to do something for her. "Oh! I'm supposed to get you a couple of dresses, ain't so?"

"*Ja.* But you got distracted." He flushed. He tended to do that sometimes. At least it happened with Beth. She might roll her eyes and cross her arms, but she never grew irritated with him. Very few people understood him the way she did.

"What did you find that interested you so much that you forgot why you were in the closet?" she asked him.

"I'll tell you what. Let's pack your suitcase, then we can deal with it. It's probably nothing exciting. I think I found a door to an attic."

Her eyebrows lifted. "An attic? We're at the top of the *haus*. The roof is directly over us."

"True." He folded her dress—purple, of course—as neatly as he could and stuffed it into the suitcase. "But the back walls of the closet slant down. There's no slant there on the roof. My guess is whoever built this *haus* put in a crawl space. It's probably empty. Or maybe home to mice or squirrels. But I'm curious."

She, on the other hand, didn't look curious at all. "*Ja*, I'll bet there's sixty years of dust and dirt and other ugly things up there. For sure, nothing has been added to it since we moved in twenty-five years ago."

He halted, the second dress in his hands. Nothing that she knew about. He considered how easily the square had shifted. As if it had been opened recently and not completely closed. He didn't want to scare her, but his mind kept returning to the fact that someone had searched the *haus* very thoroughly. The mess left behind in this room, in particular, led him to the conclusion that whoever had been searching for something hadn't found it and had reacted in anger.

Beth had said the man who had killed Joel had wanted to know where the stash was. He specifically seemed to believe that whatever the stash comprised of, it was here, in Beth's home.

Now all he needed was a way into the crawl space to test his theory.

But he didn't know that he wanted to test it with Beth present. Not only because her *daed* may have died for it. If there were some creatures living in the attic, or if it was dirty or dusty, he didn't want her to have to sift through the grime with him.

He opened his mouth to tell her it could wait when she lifted her pert nose and sniffed twice.

"Gideon, do you smell something?" She sniffed again. Her face paled. "I smell smoke."

He sniffed, his muscles tightening. "I do. It's close."

He ran to the door and felt it. "The door is not hot. We can go out here but stay close to me."

Before he left, he grabbed a couple of head scarves from her top drawer. "Cover your mouth and nose with this. We'll keep low because smoke rises."

He pulled the door. Nothing happened. The knob wouldn't turn. He tried again. The third time he wrapped his hand around it and twisted, the inside knob came off in his hands. A solid thud on the other side announced the other half of the contraption had hit the landing.

They were trapped inside the room while something burned.

Gideon spun away from the door and sprinted to the window on the side of the *haus* that faced the auction barn. Flames climbed up the trellis, licking at the base of the window. Beyond the flames, he saw the cause of the suspicious fire. A man with a thick black beard hightailed it back to his motorcycle, a gas can in one beefy hand. The can sloshed fuel over the grass as he ran.

They'd been locked inside a burning *haus*.

Gideon did not need to question Beth about what the man who shot her *daed* looked like anymore. He was staring up at Gideon, an evil grin splitting his beard open and showing a perfect set of white teeth.

The man who had shot Amos Troyer was attempting to roast them to death.

Gideon wasn't about to let him succeed.

"Beth! The *haus* is on fire. We need to find a way out."

"What about the door?" Her face told him she suspected what he was about to say.

"Someone sabotaged the doorknob. The side window is too dangerous. That is where the fire is." He ran to the window looking over the street. It was clear. But it was also twenty feet off the ground. They'd have to find a way down.

"Look. We'll go out the window overlooking the barn and climb across the roof to the tree where your *daed* hung the tire swing. We can climb down that rope to the ground."

She swallowed. "I can't see."

He strode across the room to her and took her hands. They were cold. "I know that. But I also know if we don't try, we'll both die trapped in here. We don't have a choice."

Her hands trembled in his. He tightened his grip. Leaning forward until their heads touched, he whispered a soft prayer for their continued well-being. She took a shallow breath. Nodded her head. Right. They were ready.

Still holding her hand, he led her over to the window. There was no sign of the arsonist. Nor had the flames yet reached this side of the *haus*, although by the way the trees were blowing, it would not be long before the wind fanned the flames higher, and they spread. Not to mention fires started with an accelerant were vicious and grew rapidly.

He unlocked the window and slid the glass pane up. He didn't have time to mess with the screen. Using the heel of his hand, he slapped the flimsy screen out. It fell with a loud rattle, crashing against the side of the *haus* as it went.

"That needed to be replaced, anyway," Beth said in a tight voice, trying to dispel some tension with humor.

He appreciated the attempt. It didn't work.

Now came the hard part. "Okay, Beth. I am going to help you out of the window. There is a small ledge below, about five and a half feet wide, right over where the Florida room sticks out. It's slanted, so be careful you don't slip.

When your feet touch it, I want you to sit on the roof and wait for me. Got it?"

"*Ja*. How far down is it? I'm trying to visualize it, but I've never had cause to measure it."

Not many people would.

Never had he been more grateful for his skill at measuring by sight than at this moment. Leaning out the window, he narrowed his eyes. "It's six feet and two inches down. Not bad, but it slopes, so you will slide a couple of inches."

He silently prayed she'd be able to stop sliding. "You need to get low quick. Your height, combined with the sliding motion, could make you topple over the edge."

Her mouth firmed. "I will."

They were out of time. Tendrils of thick smoke crept under the door. Within a minute, the room would be full of smoke. The window acted like a draw, pulling it farther into the room. Beth coughed.

He helped her over the windowsill, keeping his voice calm. Smoke tickled his throat. He coughed. Holding her hands, he eased her down until her feet hovered inches above the roof.

"I'm going to drop you," he warned her.

"I'm ready." Her voice didn't waver. Her trust in him shook him to the core. By now, the smoke was coming in too thick to breathe freely in the small room.

He couldn't wait any longer.

With a prayer, he let go.

EIGHT

Gideon watched her fall, heart in his throat. She hit the roof and immediately her boots began sliding. He stopped breathing. Beth dropped to her stomach and lay still on the roof.

"Gideon? Please tell me you are joining me here."

He coughed once. "*Ja*. I'm on my way. Move to the left one foot so I don't land on you."

She complied.

By now, the smoke in the room had thickened to an oily haze. For one brief second, he contemplated grabbing her suitcase. It was what they had *cumme* for. He discarded the idea immediately and swung his legs one at a time over the sill. No way could he risk retreating into that smoke-filled room. As a volunteer firefighter, he knew better than to even truly consider such a thing. As she had said earlier, they were all material possessions. Nothing that couldn't be replaced.

Neither he nor Beth were replaceable. He dropped onto the roof beside her, instantly falling to his hands and knees to cease the sliding motion.

"Now what?"

He glanced around. "Now we move to the left and catch on to the tree. It's near the corner of this roof. We'll have to crawl."

It would be tricky, given the slant of the surface.

"You'll need to direct me." She grimaced and coughed again. The smoke from the other side of the *haus* blew across their faces. Ash settled on the surface of the Florida room. "It's getting worse. The smoke."

A panicky edge tinted her words.

"*Ja*, I know. But there's still plenty of oxygen. We're outside now. That should help the smoke dissipate." He reassured her as well as he could. Then the breeze shifted, and he inhaled a lungful of acrid smoke. His lungs spasmed, sending him into a frenzy of coughing and choking.

"Gideon!"

"I'm *gut*," he rasped. "Let's move. Go to the side—left—for six feet."

She raised herself to her hands and feet and began to crawl along the roof, placing each hand down with painful care. "I can see a shadow that I think is the tree. It's hard to judge because I can't see more than that."

"Can you see the roof at all?"

"*Nee*. Nothing."

What a testament to her faith, both in *Gott* and in him. She followed his instructions without comment, trusting that he would get her to safely. It was humbling. Inch by inch, they made their way across the roof. He didn't want to say anything and add to her worry, but he could feel the surface beneath his hands growing warm.

The fire was under the roof they were on.

She needed to know. "Beth, we need to move faster. Can you feel—"

"The heat under my hands? *Ja*, I feel it. How far until I arrive at the tree?"

"Start inching your way down the incline. It's about three feet."

Three feet, two inches, to be precise. They began to move downward. Gideon switched back and forth between watching Beth's progress and keeping an eye on the flames licking at the edge of the roof. They began eating their way to the surface, greedily gobbling the wood and the insulation that was now exposed.

The Troyer *haus* was shingled with class B shingles. While these were *gut* and partially resistant to flames, they would eventually catch fire and burn. They were already starting to fail.

"You are within reach." He arrived at her side. "The fire is on the roof. Climb onto the branch three feet above your head and follow it to the tree."

Two years ago, he'd informed Amos that the tree was too close to the *haus* and should be cut down. Amos had ignored the advice, insisting that if he kept the branches trimmed, all would be well. Gideon had been more concerned about the roots digging into the plumbing or damaging the septic system, but it hadn't been his place to do more than make suggestions.

Now he thanked *Gott* for Amos's stubbornness. If he'd listened to Gideon, Beth would be forced to jump from the roof to the ground.

She stood and grabbed hold of the branch. Using both hands to keep her balance, she followed the limb to the base of the tree. Near the edge of the roof, she tripped over a shingle that had torn loose, most likely during the most recent storm.

"Beth, watch out!"

"Got it," she muttered, catching her balance.

Near the trunk of the tree, her hands connected with the rope attached to the branch. "That's the swing. Can you use it to climb down?"

Without answering, she scampered down the rope, hissing slightly when she slid. Rope burns. He waited until she was safely off the swing, then he followed the same route to get to the bottom of the swing and joined her on the grass.

"We need to run—get out of the smoke."

Taking her hand in his, he jogged with her to the edge of the road.

"Now what?" she asked.

Sirens were on the way. "Someone must have smelled the smoke or seen the fire. Help is on the way." He noticed the mare and the buggy were still in the yard. "He didn't touch the buggy. We can wait in there until the fire crew gets here."

She didn't argue. It wasn't until they were at the buggy that he realized they were still holding hands. It was true that it helped when he guided her. But he hadn't consciously done it. Holding hands with her hadn't been a calculated action to keep her safe.

He'd held her hand because it felt *gut* to have the connection.

Not liking the direction his thoughts were taking, he eased his hand out of hers and stiffly stood next to the buggy while she sat on the bench. While he'd wanted to resume his friendship with brave Beth, he'd never anticipated developing feelings beyond that with her. Nor was he sure he wanted to allow them to fester. Beth wasn't her sister, but he wasn't the same man he'd been two years earlier. He'd learned to be cautious.

Plus, Beth was vulnerable now. Her father had been murdered. More than that, he sensed her recent communication from Miriam had unsettled her. For now, he would do what he could to support her. She was alone and relied on him. He wouldn't take advantage of that. He'd offer her friendship. Nothing more. And if it was too difficult to be her friend and not develop stronger feelings, then he'd have to leave her. Again.

Shivering, Beth ran her hands up and down her arms trying to keep warm. It felt like there would be more rain today. The temperature hovered around sixty degrees. But that wasn't the only chill she felt.

Almost the moment they reached the buggy, Gideon withdrew. Both physically and, she sensed, emotionally. If only she knew what was going on inside his head. But unlike the Gideon she had known growing up, this Gideon seemed intent on keeping her at bay. Not letting her in to see what was going on inside his mind.

Wasn't that what she wanted?

It wasn't. She had no one right now except for him. But apparently, she couldn't rely on him as much as she wanted to. Oh, he would keep her safe. He had already proven that. Just as he had already shown he would put her well-being above his own.

Nee, she wasn't worried about her physical health when she was next to him. She was concerned about her heart. Gideon was a *gut* man. He was strong, and he was full of faith. He was intelligent, and she was never bored in his presence. Not to mention, how many men would allow a girl to traipse along beside them as an equal?

Her father had been one such man. Gideon had always been another. She had never felt unwelcome.

He had offered her shelter in his family home, and she knew he was sincere. But she also knew he was holding himself back from her. An inner voice mocked her, sneering that he was probably comparing her to her beautiful sister.

She shook that unworthy thought from her head.

Whether or not he was still in love with her sister, she couldn't do anything about it. But she would not continue to compare herself to Miriam. She was who *Gott* made her to be. That would have to be enough.

The sirens Gideon had noted drew closer. Within a minute, firefighters and the police were on the premises. Gideon left her and joined them. From where she sat, she could hear him telling them about going to the house to pack a bag and getting trapped in her bedroom. It was obvious by their words they did not believe it was an accident any more than she did. If only she could see their faces! When Gideon got to the part about the possible crawl space and his suspicions that whatever the killer had wanted might have been hidden in there, she put her fist to her mouth and bit down on her knuckles to hold back a cry.

Was it possible her father had been killed for something someone hid in her room? Without a doubt, if something had been there, he hadn't known anything about it. She would go to her grave proclaiming her father's innocence in any kind of scheme or evil plan. Amos Troyer had always maintained a bit of naiveté. Always, he saw the good in people. And he always believed even the most hardened criminals had the ability to change.

That was one belief he and Beth had disagreed upon.

A shape appeared in her hazy vision. As it bobbed closer, she could tell it was a person. The man called out a greeting to alert her to his presence. Relieved, she recognized Steve. He approached the buggy. Beth folded her hands in her lap and waited for him.

"Hey, Beth. How are you holding up?"

"I'm fine. Gideon got me out of the house on time."

"I'm glad to hear it. That wasn't all I was referring to, though. Do you need anything?"

He probably wanted to know how everything was going with planning the funeral and how she was holding up after her father's passing.

"I don't know. Right now, I'm taking it a minute at a time. I think I will need to contact the bishop's wife and ask her to help me plan the funeral."

Whatever else she might have said got stuck. Emotions clogged her throat.

"Hey. I know it's hard. Listen. I am having someone come over and stay with you. The fire has been contained. But since it's arson, we need to investigate. Before I go, do you know anything about this crawl space Gideon is talking about?"

She wiped her sleeve across her face, refolded her hands in her lap and took a deep breath to calm her nerves as she considered his question. The cool air smelled of smoke, but also of spring. It steadied her. Amidst the tragedy, there was life. *Gott* would provide and care for them.

"Until Gideon found the trap door in my closet, I never even knew it existed. I have no recollection of my father ever mentioning a crawl space either. Certainly, we never put anything up there as long as I can remember."

"That's kind of what Gideon thought, as well. We can't check into it until the fire has been cleared. And it's possible that whatever evidence might be there, if there is anything to be found, will be destroyed by this new fire."

She sighed, nodding her head to show she understood. Hopefully, if there was anything to be found, the fire crew had arrived early enough to harvest it. She hated thinking that whoever had done this would get away and continue his killing spree.

"There is one good piece of news," he continued.

She perked up. She could use some good news right now. *"Ja?"*

"The citizen who called 911 did so early enough that your house won't be a total loss. You will be able to rebuild. I don't know how long it will take, and I don't know if you'll ever want to live here again, but if you want to rebuild and sell the house and start over, you will have that ability."

She knew what he was trying to say. And it was something to keep in mind. He wasn't wrong when he speculated she might not ever be able to live here again. This *haus,* and all the memories in it, had been spoiled by the violence that had entered their lives.

Someone else jogged over. It was Gideon. She recognized the sound of his steps. She shook her head. How did she know they were his steps?

"Beth."

She'd been right. It unsettled her that she knew him that well. They weren't even friends still. Or were they? She was trusting him more than she did anyone else. She put the thought aside to bring out when she had time to deal with it.

"Gideon?"

"I'm going to be here for a while, helping put out the fire. I can call Isaiah to give you a ride back to my parents' *haus."*

She wanted to refuse and tell him she'd wait here until he was free. But that was silly. "I don't want to put your brother out."

"Nah. He won't mind. Anyway, he has something for you."

His smug voice informed her that Gideon was keeping a secret.

"Fine," she agreed, not without some reluctance.

"Wonderful *gut.* He's on his way."

She gasped. "Gideon Bender, you called him before you asked me."

"Ja." Before she could act offended at his officiousness, his warm hand covered hers. "Beth, you're cold. You've been through a shock. Please. It would help if I knew you were warm and cared for."

Inside, some of the ice surrounding her heart melted.

It melted even more when Isaiah Bender arrived and introduced her to Daisy. "Daisy is a border collie. She's being trained as a service dog. My buddy told me we could borrow her for a bit."

The dog pushed her nose into Beth's hands. Beth couldn't help it. She scratched the dog behind her ear, pushing her fingers through the soft fur. She'd never had a dog before.

"Will she be okay sleeping in a barn?" *Englisch* people kept dogs in their *haus*. The Amish, at least most that she knew, believed animals belonged outside. She couldn't ask her hosts to allow this gentle animal into their home.

"She'll be fine. It's spring. And her coat is thick. I will make sure she has a warm place to sleep so she won't be out in the weather unless she wants to be. I also want to teach you the commands to use."

"My vision is starting to *cumme* back. I can see some outlines now." She felt compelled to make sure he knew so he wouldn't waste Daisy's training on her.

"That's great! Glad to hear it. Daisy will help you until it's back enough that you don't need her. Dogs are great. They provide companionship and help one be more independent."

She liked the thought of that. "I'd love to have her with me."

Climbing out of the buggy, she made her way over to Isaiah's car. Daisy panted happily in the back seat.

"I waved to Gideon to let him know I was leaving with you," Isaiah informed her. The engine rumbled to life. "He looked pretty busy. We'll probably have a few hours before he gets home."

She said a quick prayer for his safety and for all those working the scene.

"*Denke* for taking the time out of your day for this."

"Not a problem. I get to see my folks. And I like being able to help my family."

He really meant it. She couldn't wrap her mind around willingly leaving the family you loved for seventeen years, but it wasn't her place to ask. Whatever his reasons were, it was clear he was happy to be reunited with his kin.

It was almost four in the afternoon by the time Gideon returned with Steve. Isaiah stayed long enough to show them all the commands for Daisy. He used German words, which were so close to Pennsylvania Dutch that they would be a breeze to remember.

After he left, Gideon asked her to *cumme* talk with him and Steve for a few minutes. She settled into a chair at the kitchen table and braced herself for whatever news they brought.

NINE

Gideon pulled out the chair next to Beth and sat down, then scooted his seat a little closer than necessary. He wanted to be near so he could comfort her if she needed it, he told himself. Deep inside, he knew he wanted to be close for himself as much as for her. If she was sad, it would hurt him.

Steve didn't comment. He was in full sergeant mode, investigating an active case. "As we already knew, the fire at your house was a clear case of arson. Gideon has given a description of the man he saw running from the scene. Our suspect was six foot one, muscular, has a shaggy black beard and mustache. He wasn't close enough to get eye color, but I think Gideon saw enough so we can get Francesca Brown to come and do a sketch."

"Oh!" Beth reached out and touched Gideon's hand. "That's *gut*! The police will be able to search for the man immediately, then. *Ja?*"

"Yes, they will." Steve cleared his throat and exchanged a glance with Gideon. This would be the difficult part. "The firefighters on scene managed to extinguish the fire before the damage was too extensive. The one side of the house, the siding and the walls will need some work. And there's a little bit of damage to the roof above the floor to your room and the two bedrooms on that side. There's also some smoke damage inside the house. No one will be able to live in the house until it's cleaned up. It's just not safe yet."

Beth nodded, her face sad. "I'm glad there's not more damage. It makes me sick that someone would do such a thing."

"Beth, there's more." Gideon kept his voice gentle.

Beth sighed. "Just say it."

A quick smile flitted across Steve's face, so fast Gideon almost missed it. He had an inkling as to what his brother-in-law was thinking. Beth telling him to say what was on his mind seemed to come up in almost every conversation they had. One of these days, he would remember that she was not one that wanted to be cosseted and have things sugarcoated. She wanted the facts, even if they were unpleasant ones.

Steve took over the narrative again. "We were able to get into the crawl space that Gideon had found. Although it looked like there hadn't been much put up there in the last two or three decades at least, someone had recently put something up there. It seems that your house became a place to hide drugs."

She gasped, her hands flying to her mouth. "Drugs? You mean like cocaine?"

"Mostly narcotics, like pills. Things sold on the streets."

Gideon wanted to comfort her. He didn't know how, though.

"I've also been in touch with Dane, the coroner. He has identified the man found in the barn."

She removed her hands from her face. "Who was it?"

"His name was Lonnie Nelson. He was a local business-man, aged fifty-three. Divorced, no kids."

"It's *gut* he had no *kinder*."

Gideon agreed. "It's awful when young ones are left without a parent."

"True." She turned her face slightly toward him. "And if he had done something illegal, that would be awful for them to live with."

Steve cleared his throat. "Well, it appeared that Mr. Nelson had a police record. He has been charged with several counts of illegal possession of drugs and with selling drugs to minors. We're not sure how he's getting the drugs. Or rather, how he got them."

Her forehead scrunched and she tilted her head. "But how would those drugs have ended up at my *haus* in my room?"

"He recently purchased the lumberyard your dad worked at. According to the foreman, your dad had been telling him about some roofing issues he wanted to take care of. Lonnie had offered to come out to the house and take a look, with the suggestion that since your dad worked there, he might be able to give him a good deal on materials. It would not shock me if Lonnie had gone there with the intent to see if he could find a place to hide some narcotics on the property. Especially right before a huge auction."

"The mud sales? Why would they be a consideration?"

Gideon hadn't heard this theory before, but his mind raced through different possibilities. "You think he was planning on using the auction barn as a front to do drug business?"

Steve nodded. "Exactly. As you said before, these events draw in crowds from miles away. How easy would it be to set up a drug exchange in the middle of all the activity with no one being the wiser? No cameras. Lots of money changing hands. Hundreds of people. And if he were on the premises, working with your dad, no one would question if he disappeared inside the house for a few minutes. It would be a perfect setup."

"But what happened? Why kill him?"

"He must have cheated someone," Gideon theorized.

"Or stole from them."

A barking dog interrupted the conversation. Steve grabbed his phone and answered it. It was a simple conversation.

"Yes."

"No"

"We can do that."

When he hung up, Gideon looked at him and waited.

"Francesca Brown will be available tomorrow at ten to see you and work on the sketch."

Gideon thought for a moment. "We should call the hospital. Dr. Lasko, the ophthalmologist, will be in tomorrow. We can do both at the same time."

Thursday morning, Beth awoke early. She blinked her eyes. While her vision wasn't completely back, she thought it was a little better than the day before. It may have been wishful thinking. Still, she could tell it was bright and sunny out. And she could see more definition to the shapes around her.

Still no facial features or fine details, but she could see enough that when she visited the barn, she could make out some small shape move to her and stop in front of her, and she knew Daisy had *cumme* to greet her. She gave the dog a brisk scratch.

Gideon called out to her. As he approached, he seemed to be holding out something.

"Are you holding something?" she asked him.

"Ja!" He seemed pleased that she'd noticed. "I *cumme* bearing coffee."

She wrinkled her nose. "Is it black?"

"Would I do that to you? I remember how you like it." She took a cautious sip of the steaming brew. Then she blinked and took another. He did remember. The bitter taste had been toned down with equal amounts of sugar and milk.

"Are you ready to go to the doctor?"

They'd called the hospital and been fortunate enough to get an eight o'clock appointment with the doctor. She'd had a last-minute cancellation. Even if she hadn't had one, she had put Beth as a high priority. It worked out well to see her before they went to the Sutter Springs Police Department. Steve didn't know how long it would take once they were there.

"I am. I think my sight is improving a little each day. I can see some definition today."

"Gut!"

Side by side, they walked back to the *haus* to eat a quick breakfast before he went to harness the mare and get the buggy going.

When it was time to leave, he came to help her into the buggy. She started to step up into the buggy, then paused. "Oh. Do you think we should take Daisy?"

"I never thought of it. But we might as well, since Isaiah went through the trouble of bringing her out."

Calling the dog, he gave her the command to get into the buggy. Daisy jumped up and sat in the back. Beth climbed onto the front bench with Gideon. It occurred to her after the vehicle was moving that they were sitting like a married couple, with her sitting on his left side. Her cheeks grew warm. She hadn't deliberately set out to sit in that way.

The trip to the hospital was mostly silent. She didn't mind that. Her upcoming visit with Dr. Lasko consumed her thoughts.

Once they arrived at the hospital, they exited the vehicle.

"What do we do with the dog?" she asked. She'd never thought about traveling with an animal before.

"She's on a leash and has a collar that clearly identifies her as a service dog. She'll go with us," Gideon responded. "You need to be the one to command her, though. After all, she's working for you. I shouldn't have done it at home."

He sounded embarrassed by the mistake.

"I can do that." She raised her voice slightly. "Daisy. *Aus*." She gave the command for Let's Go. Immediately, she saw the canine shape hop down from the buggy and lope over to her. She held the leash, and they went into the hospital.

To her surprise, no one commented on the dog at her side. Gideon checked them in. They sat to wait. "We're only a minute or two early. It shouldn't be too long."

She scoffed softly. In her experience, it always took a while to be called back, no matter what time the appointment was. To her surprise, she was called just a few minutes later.

"I'll be here when you *cumme* back," Gideon whispered. "Steve wanted me to call when you went in, so they'd have an idea of when to expect us."

She swallowed her disappointment. She'd hoped he would go with her. But she understood the urgency of what Steve requested. She gave Daisy the quiet command to lead and followed the nurse back into the patient examination room. The nurse took her vitals, then left her alone with Daisy. She shifted in her seat, uncomfortable. Dr. Lasko appeared five minutes later.

While she examined Beth, she asked questions about what she could see.

"At first, everything was dark. Now I see light, and I am starting to see the outlines of things. For example, I can see your outline, as well as that of the counter and the sink. I can't identify anything on the counter or see the knobs on the sink. Also, I can't see the door, or any facial expressions."

"That's better than nothing. Wait here."

The doctor went to the door and asked for a nurse to bring her a new cord for her laptop.

A sudden crash in the hall made Beth jump.

Dr. Lasko sighed. "Grayson, please be more careful. You almost dropped those samples."

A low voice murmured a reply. A minute later, the doctor was back, typing up notes on her computer. "Sorry about that. My cord got lost while I was traveling. I forgot I hadn't charged this overnight."

Beth told her it was fine. She'd often thought technology seemed to be handy but unreliable. She much preferred the Amish way of life. Everything she had to do to survive she could do without depending on machines or electricity.

"I must say I'm pleased with your progress. Your vision seems to be making a comeback. Do you need any more gauze pads?"

Beth squirmed in her seat. "Actually, the gauze pads got wet, and I took them off. I never replaced them."

"Hmm. I would have preferred that you kept using them. But I can't change that. I think if you keep improving like you are, your vision should be completely back to normal within a few days. Try to avoid too much activity. And be careful not to overtire yourself."

Beth nodded. Ironically, she'd had more than enough activity in the past two days but didn't think the doctor would appreciate her saying so. Instead, she thanked the woman for her time.

"I'm prescribing some eye drops you can use if your eyes feel irritated."

Sooner than Beth would have thought possible, she and Gideon were back in the buggy and on their way to the police department. That was where the real waiting began. The chief had soup and sandwiches delivered in so they could eat while the sketch artist was there. She never knew just how long it took to get an accurate sketch.

Listening to the conversation between Francesca Brown and Gideon, Beth was once again impressed with just how many details Gideon saw at a glance. Things she never even noticed. Like the fact that the man had a scar on his left cheek. His teeth were very white and perfectly spaced— possibly the result of braces. Also, according to Gideon, he had broad ears with detached earlobes. Who noticed things like that?

By the time both Gideon and Fran were done and the sketch had met his approval, Beth wanted to go home and take a nap. It had been a very long day and it was only one o'clock in the afternoon. Daisy sat at her feet, and she reached down and ran her fingers through the dog's thick coat.

Once this was all over, she might have to consider getting a dog to have around. She found she enjoyed the canine company.

"I'm done," Gideon announced. "Are you ready to go home, Beth?"

She held back a wince at the word home. "I'm ready."

Standing, she took Daisy's leash in her hand and gave the dog the command for Let's Go. Gideon took the reins in his hands and maneuvered the buggy onto the road. They had left the main part of town and were on their way back to his *haus* when he suddenly directed the mare into an extended trot.

Startled by the sudden burst of speed, Beth swayed on

the bench. Clutching at the seat with her hands, she steadied herself and yelled, "What's wrong?"

"Get down!" he shouted back. "We're being chased. He's going to hit us!"

TEN

Gideon's knuckles were white. He clamped his hands on the reins as hard as he could. They couldn't outrun the vehicle. The only thing saving them right now was the fact that they were entering a one-lane construction zone. Anyone in Ohio knew the fastest way to get on the police radar was to ignore speed limits and safety protocols at construction zones.

Once they were free of the construction, though, there'd be no chance to outrun the vehicle. He had three miles to get Beth to safety. To do all he could to ensure she lived to see another day.

Even if it meant he himself would not survive.

Scanning the area around them for any hope of escape, Gideon finally admitted to himself that there was no escape. They would have to go into the construction zone which would lock them in place. His mind raced furiously, trying to think up a viable plan. For all his intelligence, he was completely out of his depth. Following the three cars ahead of him, he merged the buggy into the single lane of traffic. The cars in front of him slowed to a halt. He stopped in the line.

The only positive he could think of was that the killer seemed to be cognizant of the surroundings and didn't want to bring any more attention to himself. He stayed in his car. A glance behind him confirmed Gideon's suspicion. A large man with a bushy black beard and dark sunglasses sat behind the wheel.

If only he could find a way to alert the construction crew. They would be able to call in the police.

But how could he do that without risking their lives as well? They already knew the man was willing to kill and had no remorse about it. If he was willing to kill Joel and Amos, what would keep him from turning his gun and the construction workers? Or, for that matter, on any of the other innocent bystanders in their cars?

He couldn't risk it. He had to find a way where if there were any casualty at all, it would be only him.

Ahead of him, the young woman holding the stop sign in front of their lane moved to the side and flipped her sign around so it said Slow. The cars started moving. Chomping her gum, probably to keep her ears from popping because of the noise-cancelling ear protection she wore, she motioned for the first vehicle to slow down.

The steady grinding and pounding of the power drill made his ears ache. The air grew heavy with diesel fumes and the odor of fresh asphalt.

Gideon glanced at Beth. She had squatted down in front of the bench as he'd asked. *Gut.* A plan started to form in his head.

"Beth!" he shouted above the noise.

She looked up at him, her expression serene despite the situation. It was at that moment that something in his chest wrenched. How had he never seen what a magnificent woman she was? Her faith put his to shame. Her ability to rely on others when necessary, yet remain strong and independent when called upon, was unique. She never complained about what she didn't have.

Not like her sister.

Beth had spent the past two days being chased, unable to see, and yet here she sat, as calm as you please, waiting for instructions.

He swallowed, praying for guidance to do well by her.

"He can't do anything while we're in construction. This will last for three miles."

She nodded. "What should we do?"

"I want you to take Daisy. She's been well trained. Tell her to guide you home, and she will. You need to get my *daed* to call Steve. Tell him where I'm at. The man they're hunting is driving a red Honda. I don't know the model. All I know is the symbol on the front."

It was too bad Ohio didn't require a front license plate. If he could have seen that, Steve could have looked up the exact car.

She blanched but didn't argue. "Daisy, *cumme*."

Panting, the border collie flowed over the opening between the inside of the buggy and the bench.

"How do we do this so he can't see me exit?"

He started to point, then realized she still couldn't see that much.

"When we go around the curve, there's several large construction vehicles parked along the side. No one is standing there. It should be possible for you to get down and run along behind them. It will take us approximately two minutes to pass them. So wait a few minutes, then give Daisy the command to go home."

"If he sees me…"

"Chances are he won't. But if he does, he'll be stuck in traffic. To get out of the vehicle with a gun when there are all these men wielding power tools and backhoes would be the height of arrogance. And poor thinking. He'd be trapped."

She didn't look convinced, but what other option was there?

"Get ready…in about ten seconds… Go!"

She called Daisy and gave her the command to jump down. Then slid off the buggy. The dog nudged her, and she clamped her hand on the leash. Gideon waited until they were behind the large tractor before moving forward. When he got past the equipment, he glanced back and saw her hiding. Glancing over his other shoulder, he saw that the bearded man remained hunched over his steering wheel. His eyes were glued to something in his hand. He lifted his hand enough for Gideon to see what it was. A phone.

Gideon glanced forward and grinned. A gleam of satisfaction and hope burst to life in his soul. The killer had been distracted long enough for Beth to escape. He blew out his breath, hard. It wouldn't take long for the bearded man to figure out that she was gone.

Gideon was almost level with the end of the construction. Near the edge, he saw a police cruiser waiting. Most likely, hoping to deter people from speeding as they resumed normal velocity. Maybe there was a way he could survive as well.

Making a split decision, the moment he passed the End Construction sign, he maneuvered the horse off the road and onto the shoulder, directly behind the cruiser. Immediately, the blue lights flashed, and the officer emerged from the cruiser. He sighed, recognizing Officer Melissa McCoy. He'd met her twice since Joss had married Steve.

The red car drove past. The driver flashed Gideon a glare, hatred marring his expression. His gaze swung to the empty bench beside Gideon and narrowed. He now knew that Beth was not with him.

Did he see her before? Or had he made an assumption?

He didn't know. Officer McCoy approached his buggy. "Gideon? It is Gideon, right?"

"Officer McCoy! We have to call Steve. He's tracking someone—a killer. The man was right behind me. In that red car. He's after Beth." He saw the license plate and rattled it off to her.

She whipped out her phone and dialed. "I don't know who Beth is. Hold on. We'll handle this."

In under a minute, Steve was on the line. "Gideon? Where are you? Where's Beth?"

"I'm just beyond the construction zone on River Road. Beth was with me. She got out with the dog and hid, and they are now traveling on foot home."

"What?"

"I couldn't think of another way to save her." Speaking fast, he repeated everything that had happened between the time they'd left the precinct until that moment. "I think the killer might be going after her now. He looked into the buggy. I think he knows she not with me."

"Okay. Listen, you continue home. If you see Beth, contact me ASAP. Got it? Do not engage with this man. He's dangerous."

"I know that. Pacifist here, remember?"

"Okay. I have two cruisers going out now. We have the description. And, Gideon, we have the identity of the man you are running from. His name is Grayson Owen. He works at the hospital in the pharmaceutical lab."

She ran as fast as she could, holding tight to Daisy's leash. When she stumbled, the dog doubled back and licked her face as if to say, "Get up. We need to move."

She hadn't wanted to leave Gideon but had no other option. They were stuck in the construction zone. If she had stayed, Gideon would not be able to make a move. He'd put her safety first. He always did. He'd have stayed and put himself in the path of mortal danger to give her a way out.

If she wasn't with him, maybe the man out to get her would leave him be. Would not harm his family or his friends.

She tripped again on the uneven ground. This time, she caught herself on her hands before sinking all the way to her knees. With a groan, she stood and gave Daisy the command to lead home.

Her side began to ache. She wasn't used to running long distances. She and Gideon used to run the length of a field. Never anything close to the number of miles from where they had been to his home. Nevertheless, she couldn't afford to stop, no matter how her side ached or her lungs burned.

She had to get to the phone and contact the police. It might be the action that saved Gideon's life. A dry sob left her throat. She desperately wanted to sit down and rest, but Gideon's life depended on her not giving in to such temptations.

She didn't know how long she had been running with Daisy in the lead when the dog suddenly brushed against her and growled. Startled, Beth froze. That's when she heard it. Something—or someone—thrashing through the trees ahead of her and to the left.

Daisy pushed at her, forcing her back. She didn't know how the dog understood that she was in trouble, but somehow Daisy sensed a threat. Beth's instinct urged her to pay attention to what the canine was trying to tell her. There was a bush right behind her. Daisy continued to push her until she was beyond the growth. The dog bit at her skirt, tugging her downward.

Did she want her to get down and hide? For a moment,

Beth didn't know what to do. Then she heard the thrashing coming closer. Whoever it was, Beth didn't think she'd be able to outrun them. Not without her vision completely returned. Even while she had been running with Daisy and tripping, she was still only running at half her normal speed, if even that.

She got down and curled up as much as she could behind the bush. Her height made it somewhat of a challenge. Fortunately, she was flexible. Daisy sank against her and burrowed into her side. At first, Beth thought the dog was hiding, too. Then she realized the sweet border collie meant to protect her from whoever was coming closer.

Peeking through the bushes, she saw the outlines of the trees and bushes surrounding her. They had taken on a creepy aspect while she ran. They swayed and moved with the breeze. Suddenly, she realized one of the trees had separated itself from the others.

Whoever had been chasing her was less than fifty feet in front of her.

Did they know she was near? Could they hear her breathing?

Beth attempted to take in slow, easy breaths. Her chest ached. Her lungs demanded she suck in gulps of oxygen now that she wasn't running. Beth fought the impulse. Any sudden, loud noise, and he'd be upon her, and she would die.

She had no doubt that she was staring at the outline of *Daed*'s killer.

Even though she couldn't see his face.

He continued marching forward, apparently unconcerned with detection. Why should he be? He was the one with the gun. She bent her head lower, praying silently for rescue that only *Gott* could provide at this late hour.

Then the sudden blare of sirens burst into the air. She'd

heard enough sirens to recognize the sound of a police cruiser. Then there were two sirens filling the air. They were close.

Voices and radios crackled in the air.

A search party! For her or the killer? She didn't know how, but somehow Gideon had alerted the police. Who else would know she needed help? She kept still, burying her face in Daisy's soft coat. The dog quivered, her muscles ready to spring into action.

The thrashing of someone running at top speed alerted her that the killer was on the run. He brushed past her hiding spot without slowing. When she lifted her head, his outline faded, merging with the trees again before disappearing. She remained where she was.

She couldn't trust that he was really gone. The voices kept moving through the area.

"Beth! Beth, where are you?"

"Gideon?" She rose to her feet. "Gideon, I'm here!"

A figure broke off and dashed her way. This one, she recognized by the graceful lope. When he approached her, she threw herself into his arms and hugged him with all her strength. Daisy pressed up against her legs.

"I thought he was going to get me. I really did."

"Beth, who?"

Steve materialized next to Gideon. "The—the killer. He was here. He was in the woods. Daisy made me hide. I don't know how she knew he was dangerous. And then I heard the sirens and the voices, and he ran. That way. I could see his shape."

Gideon kissed her forehead so quickly she might have imagined it. "*Cumme.* We should get you home. You can rest and *Mamm* will feed you. Then we need to plan."

She flushed, realizing how close they were standing. She

put some space between them and immediately missed his warmth. "What are we planning?"

Steve cleared his throat. "We know who's after you. His name is Grayson—"

"Grayson!" she gasped.

"You know him?" Steve asked, his voice tense.

She shook her head. "*Nee.* But this morning, while I was at the hospital, Dr. Lasko opened the door to the hall to ask for something. There was a crash in the hallway. I think someone dropped something. Dr. Lasko reprimanded him and called him Grayson."

"*Ja.* That makes sense. The man I described to Francesca Brown works at the hospital in the pharmaceutical lab."

"Is that how the other man, Lonnie, got the drugs?"

"Possibly. Or he stole from him."

"I can't believe he worked at the hospital the whole time."

"He did," Steve amended. "After the way he took off, with us here, I don't know if he'll be bold enough to return. I'll keep watch, just in case. My gut tells me he's on the run."

"Does that mean we're safe?"

"No," Steve informed her, his voice dripping with sympathy. "It means he'll be more desperate than ever. And possibly be out for vengeance."

The hope that had started to bloom died in her chest. They weren't safe yet. Would she ever be out of danger?

ELEVEN

Beth was asleep by the time they arrived at his parents' *haus*. Gideon was torn. On the one hand, he wanted to carry her in and let her sleep. She'd run nearly two miles before they'd found her. Not to mention the scare she'd had.

And all that after being locked in a burning *haus* the day before.

But she also needed nourishment. He had heard her stomach gurgling while she slept. Had she been awake, they might have joked about it. But the fact that she was so exhausted that she slept through it… That nearly broke his heart.

Steve stopped the car in front of the Bender *haus*. "You know Chief Spencer would authorize a protective detail for you here, if you wanted it."

Gideon shook his head. "*Denke*. I know he would. But you know my *daed*. He would see any such action as a lack of trust in *Gott*'s providence." He looked closely at his brother-in-law. "Are you grinding your teeth?"

"No. Okay, maybe. Gideon, you know I want to protect you and Beth. But I can't provide protection here without Nathan's approval. If you and Beth want to spend a few days at my place…"

Gideon put a hand up, stopping his brother-in-law from

completing the sentence. "I will never willingly put Joss and your *kinder* in danger. We are in this because we have no choice. I won't bring it to your *haus*. Joss has been through enough."

He would never forget how close his own sister came to dying so soon after they were reunited. Now she had a family to protect. It was the way the world worked.

Steve stopped arguing, although he clearly wasn't happy. "Let's get Sleeping Beauty inside."

Gideon grinned, but his heart warmed when he saw her resting in the back seat, Daisy's head on her lap. In his opinion, that dog had more than earned her place in his family. If she hadn't protected Beth, the woman he'd become so attached to would have died.

"Daisy," he called softly when he opened the back door. The dog lifted her head and wagged her tail. "Daisy, *cumme.*"

The canine remained where she was, returning her head to its position on Beth's lap.

Steve chuckled. "She's still in training. But obviously, she's decided who her handler is, and it's not you."

That was fine. He wanted her to protect Beth, not him, anyway.

He reached in and lightly shook Beth's shoulder. She jerked awake like he'd poked her with a cow prod.

"Whoa. Easy, Beth. We're home."

Her face flushed bright red. "Sorry. Overreaction."

"No worries." Steve stepped away from the car. "Daisy won't leave the car without you. You'll have to give the command."

She told the dog to jump down. Immediately, Daisy obeyed.

"Told you," Steve ribbed him. "She's decided Beth is her boss."

They made their way inside. *Mamm* had outdone herself with dinner. Unfortunately, Beth appeared too weary to do it justice. After dinner, she disappeared for the night. Steve went home and promised to return in the morning.

Friday came in with a thunderstorm around three in the morning. The *haus* shook and rattled with each clap of thunder. The lightning blazed across the sky, lighting his room up like it was the middle of the day. By the time it blew away, Gideon was wide awake.

There would be no more sleep for him.

He dressed, then meandered downstairs. He might as well get some very strong coffee and check to see if there was any damage from the storm. The creeks would be high. No doubt, there would be some flooding. Their farm would be fine, but he grabbed his pager, knowing that their department would be called out at some time during the day.

Isaiah showed up at six. "I figured you'd probably need some assistance today."

That was one thing he treasured about his family. They all did what they could to help each other out. It was never about convenience. He didn't need to ask Isaiah. His brother knew that Gideon would be called to help with the storm damage and not be able to stay at home. Gideon could trust Isaiah to look out for Beth.

The first call came in at six twenty-seven. Trees down across a major roadway. Gideon's chief stopped by on the way to the department to pick him up. He hopped into the cab willingly enough, but his mind was stuck on the fact that he hadn't had a chance to see Beth yet that morning.

After three hours, the activity settled down and he returned home. Isaiah walked out to greet him as he walked out to the garage to see if there were any chores that hadn't been done yet. The corners of his brother's mouth quivered, like he was holding in a smile.

"What's happening?" Gideon narrowed his gaze, suspicious. Isaiah had the look of a small boy hiding a secret.

Isaiah shrugged, his eyes dancing. "Nothing. I'm glad you're back. I'll be heading out now. Addie's out of ice cream."

Gideon's eyebrows climbed his forehead. "And that's important?"

"Gideon, when a pregnant woman wants ice cream, you get her ice cream. Word to the wise."

Gideon's ears were hot. But he laughed at his brother. "If you say it, I believe it."

"Oh, I do. I'll give her a kiss from you."

Gideon shook his head. People thought he was the troublemaker. But Isaiah had some mischief in his blood, too. All the chores complete, he dusted off his hands and left the garage. He couldn't wait to see Beth. When he reached the *haus*, he climbed the steps and found Beth waiting for him on the back porch. The moment he moved toward her, her face lit up. Actually, her eyes lit up.

"Beth," he breathed, barely letting himself hope, "can you *see* me?"

The brightest grin she'd ever sent his way split her face. "I can! I woke up this morning late and I ran around getting ready, when I realized I was using my eyes. They're still tired. I've used the drops Dr. Lasko gave me. But I can see."

He strode over to her and wrapped her in a warm hug. But he didn't hang on long. He wanted to see her face again. "I am wonderful happy for you!"

"*Ja*, me, too."

When *Mamm* called them in for lunch, he could barely keep his eyes off Beth's face. It glowed with joy. He'd forgotten how bright and vibrant her brown eyes could be. They sparkled with life.

The only time they dulled was when he asked her what her plans were that day.

She sighed. "I need to stop by the bishop's *haus*. It's time to plan my father's funeral, and I don't know how to go about it."

He nodded. "I'll drive you over after lunch."

Their plan was waylaid by an hour when Steve dropped by. While his news wasn't unexpected, it wasn't *gut* either. "Grayson Owen has gone underground. His apartment is trashed. He's obviously taken what he needs and left everything else. At the hospital, they reported stolen meds from the pharmacy."

"He will try to sell those," Gideon concluded.

"That is what we think. They're not sure how long he's been stealing drugs. His vehicle has been ditched. It was found on the road."

"How will he travel without a car?" Beth asked, her face set.

When Steve hesitated, Gideon borrowed her line. "Just say it."

Beth shot him a glance, eyes wide, but didn't comment. Steve met her gaze. "I hate to say it, but he'll steal a vehicle."

He wasn't saying everything. Gideon knew, and so did Steve, that he'd possibly kill someone to get the car. "Keep an eye out and keep Daisy with you. You might not need her to see for you, but she's an added layer of defense."

Beth agreed. He had an inkling that she had grown fond of the dog and wanted to keep her near, regardless of the reason.

"There's more." Steve rubbed the back of his neck. "The coroner removed the bullet from your father. It has been traced to a stolen gun that has been involved in two other unsolved killings."

"How awful!" She bit her lip. "I need to ask, when can I bury my *daed*? That should have happened today. I need to go to the bishop."

"We'll deliver the body today. Where?"

"Bring it to our barn, Steve. Mourners can *cumme* there," Gideon replied.

Steve agreed.

Steve headed back to work. Gideon strode to the barn and hitched up the mare to bring Beth to the bishop's *haus*. The bishop's wife was a kind woman. She'd be willing to assist with the difficult tasks Beth had ahead of her. Of course, she could have asked his *mamm*, but he suspected Beth felt she'd already asked too much of his family.

She didn't realize there was nothing he would not give her, or do for her, as long as it did not contradict *Gott*'s plan. Which meant he'd do anything she asked of him, for she would never look outside of what their faith allowed. Their faith was an integral part of Beth's personality.

He'd thought he was in love with her sister for so long and had nearly destroyed his friendship with the woman at his side. Now that he was beginning to see that Miriam wasn't the woman he wanted in his life, he feared he was too late.

Having her sight back overwhelmed her.

Beth had been in near darkness since Tuesday. Now that it was the middle of Friday afternoon, the brightness of the world around her dazzled and dazed her. So many colors! So many different layers to perceive.

She recalled Dr. Lasko's warning to take it easy and rest when necessary. At the time, she'd not understood. Now, she comprehended how seeing so much after the brain had been starved of visual stimulation could make one feel swamped.

At least Gideon was with her. How had she come to rely on him so much? Less than a week ago, they weren't speaking. Then this morning, when she'd discovered her sight had returned, the first person she ran to tell was Gideon.

And he wasn't there. She understood why. Gideon took his responsibilities seriously. He took great care in his call to protect and serve others. It was almost two in the afternoon when they arrived at Bishop Hershberger's *haus*. His wife, whom the community referred to as the Bishop's Edith, since Edith Bender also lived in the community, met them at the door.

"She'll have coffee ready," Gideon murmured. "I've never been here when there wasn't coffee."

"It's in the job description," she deadpanned.

He chuckled and tossed the reins down.

"Gideon! So nice to see you," Edith Hershberger called as he hopped down. Then her smile slipped from her face and her expression sobered. "Beth. I heard about your father. *Cumme*. I have coffee made."

Beth shared a glance with Gideon. She bit the inside of her lip to keep the laughter inside.

Once inside, the bishop's wife seated them and called in her husband. He came at once, a man around her father's age, his gray beard streaked with brown. His kindly face was somber now, but laugh lines spanned out from the corners of his eyes.

"Beth. I'm sorry about your father," the bishop began, his voice a deep rumble. "We knew each other for many years. He was a *gut* friend, Amos."

She swallowed to clear her throat.

"*Denke.* I need to bury him, but I don't know how." She held out her hands. "I know he should have been buried today. But the police still have his…his body. It still had a bullet in it. It's being delivered to Gideon's barn later this evening."

The bishop sighed. "Such a tragedy. Will the funeral and viewing be at your *haus*, Gideon?"

"*Ja.* Beth's *haus* and barn both have fire damage." Beth winced at the memory.

"We'll bury him tomorrow morning," the bishop decided. "You will have a pine box?"

Gideon spoke up, his tone respectful. "*Ja.* We will provide one."

"You and your father always *cumme* through for our people."

The rest of the afternoon was spent making preparations for the funeral. Beth didn't have any black dresses available, but Zeke's wife, Molly, helped her find one and alter it to fit. Gideon's whole family came together, Amish and non-Amish, and assisted. The body was laid out in Plain clothes in a simple pine box the Benders had made. The viewing was held that evening and shortened, only a single day rather than the usual two days, since he was being buried the next morning.

Beth was amazed how many people showed up, considering how little time they had to spread the news. Beth's heart was simultaneously saddened talking about her beloved parent and consoled by the amount of love shown by those who knew him.

Saturday morning, she dressed in black for the funeral. The thought flittered through her mind that she wished she could let Miriam know. However, Miriam hadn't let the family know where she had settled down.

The funeral went without incident. The women of the community had cooked a large meal for the attendees. The food smelled delicious, but Beth only picked at it. Grief sat like a ball of lead in her stomach. By early afternoon, it was done. Beth wandered aimlessly around the yard, unable to think, to plan. What was she supposed to do now? Until she'd buried her *daed*, it hadn't completely hit her that he was never coming back.

"Beth." Gideon walked up behind her. He reached out and touched her hand. "*Cumme.* Let's go for a walk."

Part of her just wanted to go back to her room and sleep. To mentally and emotionally shut down for a few hours.

But she couldn't do that. That's not how her father had raised her. And there was no one she'd rather be with in her sorrow than Gideon. "Okay."

She put her boots on and grabbed a light cloak to ward off the chill before rejoining him on the back porch. "Where are we going?"

He shrugged. "Just down the street. I thought you might need a break, ain't so?"

It did sound lovely—stretching her legs and leaving all the people and the noise for a few moments. Maybe she'd even convince him to race like she had years before. Not that racing was dignified.

They began walking, their arms swinging between them. When Gideon reached over and took her hand, Beth thought about pulling away. Looking at him, though, she decided he meant to comfort her. Right then, she sorely needed the comfort, so she left her hand in his, enjoying the closeness.

They walked for fifteen minutes or so when Gideon reluctantly suggested they turn around. Beth sighed. She wanted to disagree but had already taken up so much of his time. At least he didn't sound any more eager to go back than she felt.

She released his hand and started to turn. He turned, too, rotating in the opposite direction. They bumped into each other, and their gazes met. And caught.

She should keep going. Walk back to his *haus*. Something held her still. She couldn't hear the birds singing over her wildly beating heart.

He was going to kiss her!

She'd felt him kiss her head the other day. But that was a kiss one might give a friend. Or a sibling. The look in his gaze was not one that a man gave a friend.

The way she shivered wasn't because of the wind either.

When he stepped closer, she held her breath. She should back away. They were friends. Gideon leaned closer. Beth's eyes drifted shut.

Crack. A bullet splintered the tree branch two inches above her head.

Grayson Owen had found her.

TWELVE

Gideon's head reared back, all thoughts of kissing Beth shattered like glass.

"*Cumme* on! Run!" He grabbed her hand and tugged her away from the street. Fortunately, Beth's legs were nearly as long as his. She wore sturdy boots, rather than the flip-flops she favored in the summer, so her steps weren't hampered.

Together, they raced through the field at the end of the street and hopped over the fence near the edge, scattering chickens and an angry goose. The goose chased them for ten feet, but Gideon was more concerned about a man with a gun than the vicious fowl intent on taking a bite out of his leg.

A car engine revved on the road. Relieved that the man decided to stick to his car rather than give chase on foot, Gideon plowed into the next field, taking a detour through the barn. Beth kept pace with him the entire way, breathing like a sprinter at a marathon.

They ran for fifteen minutes. Finally, completely winded, they paused under the shade of a large oak tree.

"I haven't heard any vehicles for over ten minutes," he finally said. "I think we lost him, for now. But he won't stop looking."

"I know," Beth whispered. "He came this way to find me. Why? The police already know who he is."

Gideon squatted down and leaned back against the tree. "Revenge, maybe. Or maybe he's on someone's payroll and being forced to fix his mistakes."

She stared at him.

"I have a brother who is a marshal, one who was a bounty hunter, and my brother-in-law is a cop." He shrugged. "I hear some interesting stories and theories. Motives are not always clear. But rarely do people do evil things without something driving them."

"Why did he burn my *haus*?"

"Again, I'm only guessing, but maybe he saw us go in and needed you out of the way. Or maybe he knew the drugs were inside, but since he couldn't find them, he didn't want to leave evidence for anyone else to find."

She dropped down beside him, twisting her legs around to the side. "Gideon, I can't go back to your parents' *haus*."

His stomach roiled in his gut at her words. His head dropped forward. He didn't know how to fix this. He needed to protect her, to see this through to the end. But he understood her words. His *mamm* and *daed*, and anyone visiting the *haus* if Grayson Owen came to call, would be in peril.

"If we can't go back home, we'll have to find somewhere else." He tapped his fist against his chin while he considered his options. Slowly, he became aware that she was staring at him, her mouth open. "What?"

"I can't go back there. It doesn't mean you can't. Gideon, that's your family."

You could be, too.

Where did that thought come from? He shoved it out of his mind. The situation was serious and needed his full attention.

"*Ja*. They are. If I didn't help you, they'd be disappointed in me. I'd be disappointed in myself. Beth, you're my friend. My best non-family friend. I want to assist you."

She closed her eyes for a moment, her chin sinking to her chest. When she raised her head and met his glance again, her eyes were dry, but he felt the emotion reaching out to him. "*Denke.* But you can't let your parents wonder what happened to you."

"*Ja.* I will get word to them." He didn't know how yet, but he would. His *mamm* and *daed* had suffered losing three of their *kinder* before. He would not be irresponsible and put them through that agony again. Nor would he abandon Beth a second time, this time to outsmart a murderer alone.

She slumped against the tree, her head drifting down onto his shoulder. "Where do I go, Gideon? Where can I go where this killer won't find me?"

Tenderness rose inside him, filling his soul. He kissed her head, gently. "We'll go to Pennsylvania."

Instantly, her head popped up, reminding him of a cannonball shot from a cannon. "We'll go where?"

She had heard him. Her expression said she didn't believe him.

He smiled at her. "Pennsylvania. You have family there, ain't so?"

"*Ja.* You know I do." She shook her head. "How will we do this?"

Standing, he reached down and assisted her to her feet. "First, we will walk toward the town. I think we need to find a phone. I can call for a driver, and have someone let my parents know where we are going."

"Your brothers…?"

"I don't know how much this man knows about my family. Is he watching my brothers' *hauser*? I think our chances are better with a stranger. It will be safer for everyone."

"I didn't think about him watching your family."

Guilt crossed her pretty face.

"Please—none of this is your fault." He took her hand again and continued walking. "Let's stay off the main road as much as we can. And if we hear a vehicle *cumme*, we need to hide."

"I can do that." She turned in a circle. "So which way do we head?"

He smiled. Beth had never been *gut* with directions. Or geography. He used to tease her about it when they were younger.

"East. We need to head east toward Meadville. It's about a two and a half hour drive. We want to eventually end up on the turnpike."

Doubt stamped on her face. "That's a long way. It's already pretty late."

He nodded. "We'll find a place to stay tonight. Then we'll head out tomorrow morning. But first I need to place a call to the family."

Walking on the dirt trails, skipping the major roads, they eventually came across a couple walking their dogs. Two large golden retrievers.

"They are *Englisch*," he whispered to Beth. "I'm sure they'll have a phone."

He started toward the couple. "Excuse me!"

"Gideon!" Beth hissed, tugging at his arm. "You can't just go up to anyone and ask to use their phone."

"Why not?"

The people had paused and watched him approach, their grip on the leashes tense. The dogs, on the other hand, whined and wagged their tails. The one tried to jump up on Gideon. "Reese, heel. Snickers, come on."

Cute names.

"*Gut* evening. I was wondering if I might borrow a phone? I need to call my brother."

"You're A-mish," the man said, pronouncing the word with a long *a* sound. Gideon held in the grimace that wanted to escape. "A-mish don't use phones."

"Usually, no, but my brother is not Amish."

The man continued to dither. The woman finally rolled her eyes and scowled at the man. "Here. Use mine."

"*Denke.*" He had thought long and hard about which brother to call. Steve and Isaiah lived too close. They'd insist on driving out to get him. Micah, though, lived an hour out. He could call him and then find a ride before Micah arrived. Despite the discomfort, he agreed with Beth that they should keep his family out of it.

Dialing Micah's number, he tapped his foot while he waited.

"Micah Bender."

"Micah. It's me. Gideon."

"Gideon! Where are you? Steve called me—said you and Beth have gone missing."

"Well, *ja*. We're hiding. The man—Grayson—" he decided not to use the word killer in front of the *Englischer* "—found us. We decided to find a place to stay for the night to be safe."

He kept the conversation short. In the end, he didn't tell Micah they were traveling. Just that they were safe and would be in contact tomorrow. That way no one would try the road to Pennsylvania. He hung up and thanked the couple. They both stared at him like he had done something criminal, but he hurried Beth away.

The streetlamps had turned on. It was getting dark, and

the temperature had dropped. They had to find someplace to sleep for the night. Somewhere out of the weather.

"I know where we can go."

"The fire department?" Beth frowned at the sign.

"Sure. It's a volunteer department, so no one is here at night. I have a key. We can go in, get a few hours of sleep, then continue traveling in the morning."

She wasn't sure this was the best idea he'd ever had, but by this time, exhaustion had taken over. If she didn't sleep soon, she'd fall over. When she glanced at him and realized his face appeared hazy, fear clenched her stomach into a hard knot. She recalled the doctor warning her not to overdo it. If she didn't rest, would she damage her returning vison irreparably? She had no desire to test it.

Gideon unlocked the door and lead her quietly back into the station. A room had been set up in the rear with a couple of cots and some blankets and pillows.

"Do people actually sleep here? I thought this was a volunteer department."

He took a couple of blankets from the shelf and handed them to her. "Sometimes when there's an emergency that requires us to be on standby, it's nice to have a place to rest if we're here more than a few hours. It doesn't happen often, but we're ready if it does."

He reached up on another shelf and pulled out a small battery powered alarm clock. He set it for 5:00 a.m.

"I want us to be out of here early enough that we can still have some cover from the shadows. In case Grayson's searching still."

She hoped not. But she appreciated his caution. She didn't want to meet with a killer with a gun anytime soon.

When he pointed at the cot near the far wall, she sank

down upon it. The mattress was thin and lumpy, and the blanket was coarse. She kicked off her boots and stretched out on the uncomfortable surface and held in a sigh of sheer bliss. She'd been awake and on her feet for so long. It was hard to think of anything that had ever felt as good as lying down felt at that moment.

Despite the strange surroundings and the less than perfect bed, she fell asleep almost before she had finished pulling the blanket up over her shoulders.

When Gideon shook her awake, she opened her eyes and glared at him. "I thought you were going to let me sleep until five?"

"*Ja.* I did."

She blinked. It was still dark out. She fought with the desperate urge to close her lids again and won. Throwing the blanket off, she watched him place his in a laundry basket and did the same.

"Who washes these?"

"A couple of women volunteer to clean the hall each week. They'll clean these and any of the dish towels people use when they rent out the kitchens and the social hall."

She would love the ability to brush her teeth but didn't complain. If all went well, in a few hours, she'd be at her *oncle*'s *haus*. She'd be able to clean up and rest without constantly glancing over her shoulder.

And Gideon could return to Sutter Springs without worrying about her.

The thought saddened her. In the past few days, she'd grown accustomed to having him nearby. She would be sorry when he moved on and disappeared from her life again. Who knew how long the separation would be? Would they ever be this close again?

Dwelling on such things was unproductive.

"We need to go."

She nodded in agreement and followed him out the door. The blast of cold air on her face woke her senses better than a mug of the strong coffee he usually made. The wind bit at her cheeks and made her eyes sting. She shivered.

"Sorry, Beth. I know it's cold. Hopefully, it will be of short duration. If all goes as planned, we'll be in a vehicle with heat soon."

She kept her thoughts about the best plans and how they seldom worked the way one wanted to herself. Why ruin the morning with pessimism?

It was almost second nature for Gideon to reach out for her hand as they walked. She opened her mouth to remind him that she had her full vision back but halted. The warmth of his palm against hers comforted her. Soon, this would be a memory.

She'd cherish his presence while she could.

She silently walked beside him, listening to their booted footsteps crunching the gravel beneath their feet in the early morning.

The sunrise was shooting streams of orange and pink across the horizon when they walked into an all-day gas station. They had intended to buy a cheap breakfast and borrow the phone to find a ride. While in line, the man in front of them talked loudly on his cell phone.

"Yeah, I got both mares in the trailer. The paint's a bit jittery, but she'll settle down. It's less than three hours to the Crawford County Fairgrounds. Once she's in her stall, she'll be fine. She's young. Soon, she'll be used to the show."

Gideon's ears perked up. When he tilted his head and jerked it toward the man, raising his eyebrows, she nodded her agreement.

Outside the window, she saw a shiny black pickup truck

with an extended cab attached to a long horse trailer. From the conversation, she knew at least two horses were loaded into the trailer.

"How long is it?" she whispered.

It didn't matter, but she was curious. Gideon gave it a short glance. "Twenty-seven feet."

She grinned. She loved it when he did that. She didn't waste time wondering if he was right. He always was.

The man finished his call and slid his phone in his pocket.

"Excuse me, sir." Gideon tapped him on the shoulder.

Surprised, the man half turned. "Well, howdy, folks. I didn't see you young people back there."

She didn't feel very young this morning. Her body ached and creaked as if she'd aged sixty years in the past twenty-four hours.

Gideon quietly explained that they needed a ride to LaMar Pond. "I know that's very close to Crawford County. I heard you were going to the fairgrounds and wondered—"

"If you could catch a ride with me? Of course! But once I start, I don't plan on stopping. And I can only take you as far as the fairgrounds. I'm on my way to a horse show. I was supposed to be there yesterday, but one of my horses colicked last night."

"Oh, no!" Colic was often fatal in horses.

"It's all good," he reassured them. "I stayed up with the old girl most of the night and the vet showed up and said she's on the mend. Had to bring a different horse with me. I don't want to miss the events today."

"That would be *gut*. We can get a ride the rest of the way once we arrive."

The reality of the situation hit her. They had a ride. Someone to take them away from Grayson Owen and his murderous intent. Relief broke free inside. She fought back a surge of emotion. They weren't out of the woods yet.

Soon, though. Very soon.

Gideon paid for their food and handed her the bag. Beth moved to the truck. It would be the largest pickup truck she'd ever ridden in. There were two seats, like a car. She climbed into the cab and settled on the back seat, then peered out the window and watched Gideon assist the man carry his supplies. She saw him offer the man money for gas, to pay their way. The gentleman waved it away.

"Save your money. Why pay me to drive where I was already heading? I'll tell you what, this is a boring trip usually. No scenery. The land is flat as a pancake. It will liven things up having a couple of young folks to chat with."

She grimaced. He had no idea how eventful a trip with the two of them could be. She hoped he never had the opportunity to find out.

THIRTEEN

Gideon settled into the passenger seat of the truck, giving Beth a quick glance to ensure she was well. She reassured him with a gentle smile. Weariness shone on her familiar face—despite the few hours of sleep they'd managed to snag at the volunteer fire department—etched into new lines carved on either side of her mouth. The dark hollows under her rich brown eyes had deepened and appeared almost purple, like bruises.

He'd give much to see those signs of fatigue and sorrow erased permanently.

Yet sorrow was life. He couldn't protect her from all of it. Even had none of this happened, she would have faced it in another situation. Feeling pensive, he faced the front. His mother's face swam to the front of his mind. Micah would do his best to reassure his parents, all the while trying to locate him, but he knew they'd still worry. It hurt, knowing he was the cause of such concern. But he honestly didn't see how it could have been avoided. He'd rather them worry briefly than know that Beth had been killed because he'd left her on her own.

The man who'd so generously offered them a lift hefted himself into the driver's seat, the spurs on the back of his cowboy boots jangling. He tossed a cowboy hat onto the seat beside him.

"Name's Ted. Ted Silvo."

"Nice to meet you. I'm Gideon. This is my friend Beth. We're grateful for the ride."

"Not a problem. Me and my horses take part in the horse shows all over this part of the country every spring."

Beth leaned forward. "You ride Western, *ja*?"

Gideon's eyes widened. He hadn't ever thought about different riding styles. This was new information for him. Always eager to learn, he fastened his attention on the conversation.

Ted laughed. "You know about horse riding? I don't mean to be nosy, but I always heard Amish don't ride horses."

She smiled. "Most Amish that I know don't. Our horses are used to pull buggies and work in the fields. Although some Amish keep equipment for that. My cousin, Thomas, is a farrier in Pennsylvania. Many of his clients do horse shows. He told me some ride Western, some do English riding, which I guess is very different—"

"Yep. English riders wear different outfits and helmets—more sedate, rather than the showy Western costumes and cowboy hats. You'll never see an English rider with sequins, but Western riders love the flash."

"And he also said some do jumpers?"

Her pitch rose at the end, making it a question.

"There are quite a variety of styles. Not all horses can do them all. For example, quarter horses make the best Western show horses. My daughter does English and prefers warmbloods and thoroughbreds. It all depends on what kind of events you want to do."

Gideon shook his head in wonder. It had never occurred

to him to think about the sporty side of horses. To him, they were made for more practical uses.

"How many are in the trailer?" he asked.

"I have two of my girls with me today."

By girls, Gideon assumed he meant mares.

Ted adjusted his mirrors and then moved into the lane to merge onto the interstate. "More traffic than I expected at this time of day."

Gideon frowned. There were a fair number of vehicles on the road. It would get worse once they hit Cleveland. He glanced at the clock. It was Sunday, so the chances of getting stuck in any kind of rush hour traffic were slim.

He stretched his legs out in front of him, enjoying the rush of warmth pumping out of the heater vents. Then he thought of Beth. Dismayed, he twisted around to see her.

"Are you warm enough, Beth?"

"There are blankets next to you, miss. Go ahead and use them. They're clean. I always have my wife pack me a few so I can catch some sleep if I get tired when I travel."

She smiled. "*Denke*. I'm comfortable."

Gideon furrowed his brow. Was she really? Or just being polite.

"Get that look off your face, Gideon Bender. I'm fine. Honest. I would tell you if I wasn't. I've never lied to you, ain't so?"

It was true. If asked, Beth would tell the truth, even if it wasn't what you really wanted to hear. Most of their acquaintances learned quick enough not to ask her opinion unless you truly wanted to hear it. He had to admire that quality. Too many people said what they thought you wanted to hear, leaving you in the dark until it was too late.

Ted muttered, his voice thick with irritation. He glanced

into his rearview mirror, then his side mirror and back to the rearview.

Gideon shifted to have a look in the mirror at his side, his instincts on high alert. In the back, Beth tensed.

"What is that idiot doing?"

Beth's hand moved to grip Gideon's shoulder. He put his on top of it and squeezed. "What is wrong?"

"Oh, nothing." Ted snorted in disgust. "Some guy in a muscle car is driving like he got his license from a cereal box. Seriously. He is going way too fast. He pulls into the passing lane, slows down, then speeds up. He keeps going between vehicles."

Gideon's gaze caught Beth's, wide with trepidation. They were thinking the same thing. This wasn't a random reckless driver. Somehow, Grayson knew they were in one of these vehicles.

Had he been asking people if they had seen an Amish man and woman? There had been plenty of people at the gas station. Someone might have heard them asking about a ride. All he'd need to do was figure out which vehicle they were in.

He didn't want to consider what he'd do if he saw them.

"Beth," he started.

She ducked down into the back, sitting out of view.

Would Grayson recognize him? Many *Englisch* seemed to think all Amish men looked alike. And the man's attention had always been focused on Beth. She was his target, after all. Suddenly, he realized they'd left Ted at a disadvantage.

Ted, who had offered to assist them.

"Ted, there's a chance this man may be after us."

"You," Ted scoffed. "What could you have done?"

Beth's voice floated up from the back. "My father was

murdered on Tuesday. I saw his face. Now he's after me, too."

Ted's mouth fell open. His eyes bulged in their sockets. "This is like on television!"

Gideon blinked, startled by the reaction. "If you want, you can slow down, maybe stop on a ramp, let us off."

Ted snorted and swerved onto the ramp to merge onto the interstate. "Not likely. Folks, I don't know what most people would do, but I don't believe in leaving others to suffer if I can help."

Gideon swallowed. "It's not that easy. You are taking a risk, if this is that man and he's searching for us."

"Life is a risk. I still accept it. That's my Christian duty. God doesn't promise that living like Christ will make you safer."

He couldn't argue with that.

"Did he follow you?"

Ted glanced in the mirror. He pushed down on the gas and sped up. "Well, I don't know if he's following me. Not yet. But yeah, the car is behind us now. About three vehicles back."

Gideon hunched down and leaned closer to the door to see through the side mirror better. At first, he couldn't see anything that screamed danger. Then the vehicles shifted. A car roared into place directly behind them. As the car came too close to the right shoulder, he got a partial glimpse of the man driving.

Enough to see a horrifyingly familiar black beard.

He'd found them.

"It's him," he grated out. "I'm so sorry, Ted. I truly thought we'd be safe once we reached the interstate."

"Not your fault." Ted's teeth were clenched. He pushed

the gas pedal again. The truck engine revved and the needle on speedometer slowly climbed.

A truck pulling a trailer would never outrun a car like the one chasing after them.

Ted pulled out his phone. "I'm dialing 911."

Gideon braced his hand on the dashboard. "Tell them you're being chased by Grayson Owen, a man wanted by the Sutter Springs Police Department. My brother-in-law is Sergeant Steve Beck. He'll verify everything I've said."

It was a testament to how serious the moment was that the man didn't raise an eyebrow at hearing the Amish man in his truck was claiming an *Englisch* cop as a brother.

Ted dialed the number. The call went through on speaker phone.

"911. What's your emergency?"

"My name is Theodore Silvo. I'm pulling a horse trailer on the Ohio Turnpike." He glanced at the side of the road, then rattled off the mile marker and the make and model of his truck. "I'm being trailed by a car. My passenger is Gideon Bender—"

"Sergeant Beck's brother-in-law?" the 911 operator asked.

"This is Gideon. *Ja.* The man chasing us is a known murderer—Grayson Owen. I have Beth Troyer with me."

"Stay on the line. I'm notifying the police now. Are you in safe?"

Why would they call if they were safe? Obviously, if a killer was chasing them, the answer was negative.

Before he could respond, the driver's side mirror shattered. Beth screamed.

"*Nee!* We are not safe!" Gideon yelled. "He is shooting at us."

The police would never get there in time. He'd led Beth and Ted into a death trap.

* * *

Beth watched the horror dawn on Gideon's face an instant before another shot rang out. The trailer began to swing. Each swing pulled the truck along.

"He's shot one of the wheels out!" Ted hollered. "I have no control! My truck's going to crash!"

Behind her, the horses shrieked in panic. Her heart wrenched inside her chest. So much pain and fear, all caused by one man bent on destruction. She lifted up a prayer for help, but her prayer was distracted.

Glancing back, she watched the other vehicles slow down as the drivers noticed the precarious movement of the trailer. It swerved to the left, dragging the rear of the truck with it. Then it swerved back to the right. The swings were small at first, but each one grew larger. It was like watching a pendulum. She'd seen a truck hauling an open trailer carrying lumber crash once. It had started swinging slowly until it had finally gone out of control.

"Negative tongue weight," her *daed* had told her. "Too much weight in the trailer, not enough in the truck. When it swung, the truck wheels left the pavement. Nothing the driver could do at that point."

The next swing sent the edge of the trailer off the shoulder. It swiped the guardrail, leaving a large dent. The truck was all over the road now. Then suddenly, the trailer swung so hard, the truck hurled into a full turn, whirling as the trailer pulled it along. The trailer shot across the center of the interstate, smashing through the guardrail on the opposite side and coming to a halt lengthwise across both lanes of the interstate for the opposite direction. The truck lurched and tilted, sliding and twisting over the shoulder and rolling onto its side. The seatbelt jerked tight, digging into Beth's chest and abdomen, holding her in place.

The 911 operator was calling to them, asking for their situation.

"The driver is unconscious," Gideon's voice rasped. "Beth?"

"I'm okay." She sniffed. "I smell gas."

The operator's voice took on a new urgency. "You have to get out of there. If gas is leaking, the truck might explode."

Someone pounded on the front window. She screamed, expecting to see Grayson peering in on them. A group of people from the other cars surrounded the truck. Several of the men were holding on to truck.

"What are they doing?"

"Truck's tippy," Ted answered, his voice groggy. The relief hit her. He'd regained consciousness.

"Tippy?" She'd never heard that term before.

"Unstable." Ted blinked at her. "If they let go, the truck will roll. We have to get out."

Several more men joined those holding on to the truck. Two more climbed on top to the truck and wrenched the passenger door open. "Are you all okay in there?"

A man in a baseball cap and scruffy beard called down, "I'm an EMT. We're trying to get you out."

Another man joined him. "Anyone hurt?"

Beth shook her head when they looked at her. "I'm fine."

Gideon answered that he was well, too. "Ted? You were unconscious for a minute."

"I'm fine. It's my horses I'm worried about."

Beth craned her neck and saw a woman walking toward the trailer, carrying a bag of some sort.

"That's my wife. She's a vet. Small animals, mostly, but she knows horses. She'll check them out," a man said.

"The dispatcher told us to get out of the truck," Gideon said. "We are smelling gas."

"Same." The first man looked at them. "I think we should get you out first, then we can reach the girl. Her door is smashed shut."

Gideon, she knew, wasn't happy about leaving her trapped, but he agreed. They didn't have time to argue. Not only was she smelling gas, but who knew when Grayson would make another appearance. She had no idea where he had gone after shooting out the tire, and that disturbed her.

Five minutes later, Gideon was out of the truck and joining the crew working to get her and Ted free. Arms reached in and cut her seat belt away. She fell deeper into the cab toward the door lying on the ground. She pulled herself up and stood Her boots crunched on broken glass. When Gideon reached in, she grasped his hands and he lifted her out, then clasped her to him in a brief hug before he passed her to another bystander.

Sirens signaled the arrival of the police. An ambulance followed. She looked around. Cars lined the shoulder, even though the truck was in the center. On the opposite side, the traffic was backed up. A man wearing a neon vest was directing traffic into a slow single line. The vehicles were able to pass on the shoulder.

That would take forever.

Glancing back, she saw Gideon helping to get Ted from the truck. The horses were still in the trailer.

She darted across the center of the interstate, avoiding piles of glass and debris, and ran to the trailer. The panicked mares kicked at the walls.

Pity for the beasts surged in her chest. She joined in the effort to pry the bars locking the main doors off so the horses could be released. One of the men ran to his truck and grabbed a toolbox. Soon, the air was filled with the sound of the bar being smashed away. Two minutes later, the door flew open. The horses were frenzied. The vet approached the first mare with a soothing voice. When she cut the bridle and lead rope, the horse screamed and backed out of the trailer. When her hooves hit the road, she reared, then galloped away. Soon the other mare was out, but this one remained closer.

Flashes of light startled her. A crowd of people surrounded them, taking pictures on their phones. The fire department had arrived and had immediately moved to soak up the gas spill. That was a relief. How would they get all these people out if there was an emergency?

Ted had been removed from the truck and placed on a stretcher. The paramedics were working on him. Poor Ted. All he'd wanted was to go to a horse show.

The paint mare had been caught and was being led back.

"Your wife is on her way," a police officer told Ted. "She's bringing a new trailer for the horses."

A paramedic approached her. "Miss Troyer?"

She faced him, straightening her lopsided *kapp*. *"Ja?"*

"Your friend—" he gestured toward where Gideon stood talking with the emergency crew "—he told us you'd recently suffered a head injury and asked us to make sure you were all right."

Her eyes caught Gideon's across the distance. She rolled hers at him. He grinned but made a motion to go on.

She followed the paramedic back to the ambulance. Patiently, she answered their questions and sat through being prodded and poked yet again. A light shone in her eyes. She had been worried that all the excitement might have injured her newly returned vision, but they didn't act concerned, so she didn't bring it up.

"You'll have a few bruises. Nothing looks too serious.

Of course, it would be wise to let us bring you to the hospital to get a complete examination."

"*Nee*, I don't need one. *Denke*, but I'm fine." There was no way she was going back to the hospital. She needed to get to her family, and she needed the police to catch Grayson Owen. That was all she required.

Then her head turned, and she found Gideon again.

Nee, that wasn't all she needed to be happy, but she knew better than some that not all wishes came true. She and Gideon had reformed their friendship in the past few days. And although at times she sensed that his affections had changed in nature, it was probably nothing more than the intense situation that had thrown them together. She couldn't—wouldn't—expect anything permanent to happen. Once she was back with her family, he'd go his own way, and she would go on hers alone.

It brought no comfort admitting it. But she was a practical woman. She had to be.

She thanked the paramedics and stood to leave. They tried once more to convince her to go with them, but she smiled and shook her head. She left to go to Gideon.

She passed a car with a flashing light—one of the EMT's vehicles. A muscled hand snaked out and caught her arm. It dragged her behind the car. And brought her face to face with the man from all her nightmares.

Grayson Owen had found her.

FOURTEEN

Gideon glanced around. Where was Beth? He'd seen her less than five minutes ago. She'd been with the paramedics. He saw them packing up their gear and strode over to them. Maybe they'd know. Every instinct screamed at him to hurry. He hadn't forgotten that the reason they were in this mess was that Grayson Owen had attacked them, again, and then vanished before the police had arrived.

"Have you seen Beth?" He approached them, keeping his voice steady with supreme effort. Worry wrapped itself around him, holding him in a chokehold. "Do you know where she went?"

"Yes, we checked her out. She had some bruises, but she refused to go to the hospital for further exams."

That's what he would have expected her to do. Still, they hadn't answered his second question. "Where did she go?"

The paramedic shrugged, offering him a sympathetic smile. "Sorry. After she left us, I didn't watch where she went. But she's got to be around here somewhere, right?"

The other paramedic nodded. "I doubt she'd take off on her own."

That was the problem. She wouldn't take off on her own, but that didn't mean she was here. He had to find her.

Gideon spent the next ten minutes asking everyone he

found if they had seen the young Amish woman. No one had seen her in the last twenty minutes or so. Urgency heightened, and his adrenaline kicked into high gear.

Beth was missing and Grayson had yet to be found. While he prayed he was wrong, Gideon feared the two were connected.

He had to find her.

Across the interstate, a familiar police cruiser pulled in along its shoulder. Dodging onlookers and emergency personnel, Gideon raced to Steve's car.

"Beth's missing," he blurted, his pulse hammering in his ears.

Steve stepped out of the vehicle and opened the back door. Daisy hopped out. "I stopped by the house last night when you two went missing. Micah called me. He's searching for you, too. I called him when we heard about the wreck. He's with your parents, and Isaiah is on his way here."

Steve didn't ask what he thinking, but the implication was clear. Gideon shrugged it off. The past no longer mattered. Nothing mattered except finding Beth. Alive.

"Why is Daisy here?"

Steve pulled out a purple dress. Beth's dress. "She's more than a service dog. She has been trained to help Beth. She'll help us find her." He held out the dress to the dog to sniff. When he ordered her to find Beth, Gideon's heart leaped into his throat. Was it possible?

Daisy sniffed the piece of clothing, then barked once before dashing across the road. The two men followed her as she tracked the scent. She led them on a chaotic path. Finally, she stopped and whined.

"Her trail ends here," Steve said. He squatted down. "These tracks are fresh. It looks like someone backed up here. They backed off the ramp."

"He has her. Grayson Owen. He took her."

The only reason he hadn't killed her here was because there were too many witnesses. That wouldn't stop him for long.

"We need to put out a BOLO for her."

Gideon nodded. Having a brother-in-law in law enforcement, he was familiar with much of the jargon they used, including the anacronym for Be On the Look Out. He listened as Steve called it in. Would they find her in time? She'd been gone for half an hour. That was too much time.

"Gideon!"

Spinning, he raced toward Isaiah's voice and skidded to a halt beside his brother.

"Where's Beth?" Isaiah asked.

Fresh grief and panic surfaced as he told his brother about her disappearance. His eyes stung. He had to find her. *Please, Gott! Why bring us together and then take her from me?*

"Hey, man. I'm here. I'll help you find her."

Isaiah's hand landed on his shoulder.

"He will kill her, Isaiah. That man plans to kill Beth. I have to find her."

He stopped himself before he said, "I love her," but he knew that both Steve and Isaiah already knew that. Thinking of a future without Beth when he thought she'd be safe in Pennsylvania had hurt. He didn't know how he'd move forward if she were no longer in the world.

When had she become the most important person in his life? For so long, all he'd wanted had been Miriam.

Nee. Even when he thought he loved Miriam, Beth had been the one he really talked to. She had been the one person who always understood him. He had never needed to hide with Beth.

And she was in danger. He had to find her.

"Look, my car is parked on the ramp. We'll get off the interstate. Steve will get in his car and search, too. And I know Micah will join us in searching. We all have phones. Anyone hears anything, call the others."

Steve nodded. "The department has mobilized. They are actively looking. They know we have a hostage situation."

Hostage. Bile rose in his esophagus. The bitter taste filled his mouth. He swallowed it down, fought for control.

Running beside Isaiah, he kept the communication between himself and *Gott* wide open, calling on his heavenly Father with all his strength. Human skills would not be sufficient. If they were to get Beth back, they'd need the saving power only *Gott* could provide.

It took less than five minutes to arrive at Isaiah's car, but it felt like an eternity. Gideon hopped in the passenger seat and quickly yanked the seat buckle across his torso. Isaiah jumped in behind the steering wheel and started the ignition.

"Go, go, go," Gideon urged his brother. Fear slammed through his veins. For the first time in his adult life, he couldn't think. All he could do was feel. He wrestled the fear back. He would be no good to Beth or anyone else if he couldn't get his emotions under control.

She must be so scared.

He dug the heels of his hands into his eyes, holding the tears that threatened to fall at bay. He hadn't cried since the day Isaiah returned to the family. That was two years ago.

It wasn't often that Gideon was overtaken by strong emotion.

"I'm going, little brother. I'm going as fast as I can." Isaiah's jaw was taut. He knew what Gideon was going through. Isaiah had willingly put his life on the line for others many times. First in service to his country when he joined the military, then during his years as a bounty hunter. When he had met his wife, Addison, he had put his life and his reputation on the line to protect the woman he loved.

If anyone understood what he was going through right now, it was his brother.

Isaiah's phone rang. Unlike Steve or Micah, Isaiah didn't have his phone connected to his vehicle by Bluetooth. That feature had broken unfortunately. He fumbled with the phone and handed it to Gideon. Gideon answered it and pushed the button to put it on speaker.

"Steve. Have you heard anything? Anything new?"

He held his breath, waiting for the news that would either devastate him or bring him hope.

"I think she's been seen."

Gideon fell back against the seat at his brother-in-law's words. They could only mean one thing. Beth was alive.

"Where?" Isaiah barked harshly, rage shivering in his voice.

No one messed with Isaiah's family. Gideon knew that Isaiah's fury at injustice ran deep and had its origins in events that occurred in his youth.

"Heading toward North Gate River."

"That's not far from here." Gideon mentally calculated. "We can be there in eight minutes. Seven if Isaiah goes a little faster."

"I'm on my way. I'll let Micah know."

Steve disconnected the call.

Gideon couldn't sit still. He found himself rocking in his seat and forced himself to stop. The energy rushing through him needed to be released somehow. He alternated between rubbing his palms on his legs and pounding his fists against his thighs.

"Hold on, little brother," Isaiah ground out. "I think I can push this bucket of bolts a little faster."

Isaiah pressed down on the gas, and the car flew forward. Normally, extreme speed made Gideon a bit nauseous, as he was used to the comfortable velocity of traveling by horse-drawn buggy. Right now, his brother could go as fast as he wanted, and he'd not complain. He barely noticed the discomfort brought on by the motion of the vehicle as it hurtled around curves.

"Hold on, Beth. We're coming. Just a little longer."

Beth's stomach lurched when the car dodged another vehicle and flew around a curve, bounding off the curb. The angry driver honked his horn, waving his fist.

He didn't know how fortunate he was that Grayson ignored him. She kept her face turned away from the back seat. She'd made the mistake of glancing back when he'd first forced her into the car. The sight of the body lying in the floorboard, the woman's wide unseeing gaze, sickened her.

The only reason she was still alive, she was sure, was that they had too many witnesses on the interstate. He'd not wanted to risk taking her out while so many police officers were present on the streets. Even as they put distance between them and the accident he had caused by shooting out the horse trailer tires, they continued to pass emergency vehicles and cruisers. Several unmarked police cars with lights flashing on top of the dashboards passed them, as well.

"This place is crawling with cops." He swore viciously, glaring at her as if she were responsible for the presence of law enforcement.

Gratitude flooded her soul. That presence, while it

hadn't kept her from being captured, had made him hesitate to end her life. For now. But she knew she was down to minutes. Soon, he'd feel safe enough to risk killing her.

She rubbed her hand over her wrist. She was sure it was bruised, thanks to the hard grip he'd kept on her while dragging her away from Gideon. She had felt as though he were crushing her bones to dust under her skin. The pain, though, had served a purpose. It had kept her from giving in to the panic that threatened to consume her.

She needed to be prepared to run if she had the opportunity. Knowing it wasn't likely, she sent up a prayer for Gideon and his brothers to find her. It was the only hope she had left. But regardless, she was ready to die, if it was *Gott*'s will. But she would not make it easy. She intended to do her best to get free and return to Gideon. If she could.

The man beside her eased his right hand off the steering wheel and pulled the gun out of his pocket. She held her breath. Would he shoot her in the car while he drove? She already knew it didn't bother him to end someone's life, but she hoped it would be too risky to drive with a dead person slumped against the window for anyone to see.

He held the gun but made no movement to use it on her.

She released her breath in a slow steam, hoping to not draw his attention to her.

"Another cop," he muttered when a cruiser roared past, sirens blaring. "They are all out today. But they'll be too late to save you."

He didn't say anything more. Grayson didn't bother to talk to her. Mostly, he muttered to himself. She was not about to ask him questions. If she could make him forget her presence for a few miles by remaining silent, she was *gut* with that.

The sun was high in the sky now. It had to be close to

lunch time. Her stomach growled, but even if he handed her a gourmet meal on a clean plate, she would be unable to eat a bite. Or keep it down. A woman looked up from her cell phone as they passed. Her eyes met Beth's and widened. Beth noticed the hearing aids in her ears. While Beth watched, she looked back to her phone, then up at Beth again.

She made a gesture at Beth. Her community had a couple of deaf people. She had seen a few signs over the years. Eyes widening. She realized she knew what the woman was saying.

Help you.

I will help you.

Was she calling the police? They had to have a way to let people know when they were looking for someone.

The phone in the console started beeping rapidly, a shrill alarm of some kind. An automated voice began speaking. It took only a second to realize that the voice was talking about her. They were looking for her and Grayson.

Furious, Grayson began to curse. "They've put out a BOLO. I can't continue on the main street. Too many cameras."

He twisted the steering wheel, then cut the wheel to the right and careened across the outside lane, cutting off an oncoming car. The other driver swerved to miss him. The bumper caught their tire. Grayson straightened the wheel and kept going, moving onto the side road. Five minutes later, they were pulling onto another street. This one was a two-lane street. It was headed for North Gate River. Beth had been on this road many times.

The car made a strange scraping sound. The vibrations under her changed. In fact, the feel of the car, and how it sat, seemed different.

Slamming his open palm against the steering wheel,

Grayson pulled over. He stomped out of the vehicle and around to her side. He yanked her door open, then jerked her out of the vehicle.

The back tire was so flat, it looked like it had melted into a puddle of rubber on the road. It must have been damaged when he'd cut off the other car. She attempted to tug her arm free, but he wasn't about to let her go.

Beth held in a scream as Grayson twisted her arm behind her back. He hit the back of her head.

"Stop that."

He didn't promise to let her live if she did. She knew that was not in his plan for her. Pushing her along, he forced her to move toward the river. The pain in her arm lessened, but it still ached.

Everything ached. Her heart especially.

In the distance, she heard the river. It was not a small babble. The body of water was flowing fast. Too fast for anyone to take a canoe or a kayak on it. The grass along the road seemed soggy. When she stepped on it, there was a distinct squelching sound. It was completely saturated from all the recent rain.

There was a large branch in the way. It had probably fallen during the last storm. When he pressed her forward, she had to hop to miss the branch. Her sudden movement unbalanced her captor.

His grip loosened.

She ripped her arms free and tore off, her feet sinking into the muddy bank as she tried to put as much distance as she could between herself and the man who planned to end her life. He shouted. Heavy footsteps stomped behind her, getting sucked into the mud just as she had.

He couldn't run any better than she could. Maybe she could outrun him.

A bullet rang out. She screamed and pushed herself to run faster. If only she could make it to a cop. They'd been everywhere ten minutes ago. Now there wasn't a single vehicle in sight.

Up ahead of her, she could see a one-lane bridge. She didn't want to go over it. It would lock her in to a small area, but she had no other choice. Grayson continued to gain on her. There was no way she could turn back and head in the other direction.

She zigzagged along the riverbank, dodging branches and uneven ground. She was too close to the water.

Another shot rang out. Heat slashed across her upper arm, followed by searing agony. She cried out and tripped. Her feet slipped. Flailing to catch her balance, she half turned. Grayson charged toward her. Stepping back on the treacherous terrain, Beth's foot flew out from beneath her. She teetered for two seconds before crashing down into the raging river. The water gushed over her head.

Had she gotten away only to meet her death in the river?

FIFTEEN

Gideon sucked in a breath, shock zipping through him. Nothing could have prepared him for the sight of the woman he had fallen in love with tipping backward out of his line of vision and into the swollen river. If he lived to be a hundred years old, he would never forget those few seconds. Sitting in the car wasn't going to help her.

Gideon slammed his hands against the dashboard. "Stop the car!"

Beside him, Isaiah grunted his agreement. He spun the wheel in a move that would make a race car driver proud and crossed the center line, nearly driving into the guardrail on the other side of the road before he straightened the vehicle and parked it parallel to the rail. He stomped his foot down on the brake pedal. The tires squealed and the car shimmied.

Gideon threw open the passenger door. An oncoming car swerved to miss it, its driver honking its horn. He barely noticed. All his focus was on the place where he had last seen Beth before she'd fallen.

"Beth!" Gideon shouted. He leaped from the vehicle raced to the edge of the bank. Isaiah had the car in Park and pounded up behind him. Breathing hard, he scanned the choppy water for any sign of her. Twenty feet away,

Beth surfaced, spitting out water. Her *kapp* was caught on a branch and yanked off her head. She gasped out a soft scream, then was pulled under again. Beth was strong and wiry. But he had seen Grayson shoot at her right before she toppled over. She was injured. Plus, the river current was too rapid for her to swim toward him.

She was alive, he reminded himself. But for how long? He needed to get help, fast.

Then he remembered Grayson and shifted his stance. Grayson raised his arm again, ready to fire into the current. At the woman Gideon loved. Fury like he had never known rose inside him. Gideon started toward the man, knowing in his heart he would never get to him before the shot was fired. He forced himself to move at top speed, but there was too much resistance form the soft ground. His shoes sank into the mud with each step.

A blur of motion on his right made him spin in time to see sweet Daisy, her mouth stretched wide in a fierce growl, charge at Grayson. The man dropped the gun he had been aiming at Beth and covered his face with his arms, backing up. The border collie didn't give Grayson the chance to escape. With one powerful bound, she was on him, her teeth fastened on his left arm. They went down and landed in the moist dirt. Her growls sent shivers down Gideon's spine. In all the time she had been with them, he'd never heard her sound so terrifying.

Grayson had threatened someone Daisy had been charged to protect. Gideon wouldn't underestimate her again. He had been so focused on Beth and Grayson that he had not noticed when Steve had pulled up with the canine in tow. The siren was off, but the lights were on, alternately splashing blue and white on the landscape.

Grayson screamed, but Gideon didn't know if it were

from pain, fear or anger. Maybe all three combined. He didn't care. Beth was no longer in his sight.

Steve rushed past him and called Daisy off. The canine released Grayson and backed away. When the killer moved, she growled. He stilled. Then she tossed a doggy grin at Gideon as if to say, "He's not going anywhere."

Gideon had waited long enough. Steve had Grayson on his stomach and was reading him his Miranda rights. Gideon spun on his heel and raced back to Isaiah's car. Isaiah didn't need to be told what was happening. He had the car started and was backing up before Gideon's door was shut.

"We'll head downstream," Isaiah informed him. "That way we can get ahead of her. That's the only way we'll be able to get to her and pull her to safety."

He was correct. Gideon knew he was correct. The knowledge that they had to drive past Beth to save her rankled. At the moment, all his vast intelligence and his skills at analyzing data were at odds with his heart. He had to put his emotions aside and force himself to think.

"A normal river current will travel about 3.5 miles per hour. This one is going twice as fast. So, say 7 miles an hour. She's been in the water for five minutes. That's about 1.16 miles for every ten minutes in the water."

Isaiah flicked his blinker on and sped past a slower vehicle, maneuvering back into their lane before a curve. "So, if we go to the two miles point, we should see her before she goes past."

He hoped so. "Can we get there before she's been in the water under ten minutes? If we go over ten, we'll need to travel farther."

The longer she stayed in the water, the slimmer her chances of making it out alive were.

This road had never felt slower, not even when travelling it in a buggy pulled by *Daed*'s elderly mare. Thankfully, this particular route didn't see a lot of traffic. Otherwise, the situation might be more fraught. Much more.

"Give me your phone." He held out his hand and wiggled his fingers for Isaiah's cell phone. He had never appreciated his brother's practical nature more than when he simply handed him the phone with no questions. Gideon took the phone, only then noticing that his hands were shaking, and dialed 911. He put the phone on speaker so Isaiah could hear it, as well. Gideon closed his eyes, forcing all outside stimuli away so he could listen to the dispatcher's voice over the blood pounding in his ears.

"911. What's the nature of your emergency?"

Blowing out a breath, he opened his eyes to glance at the mile marker on the side of the road, then moved his gaze to the readings on the dashboard. He thumped his closed fist on his right knee. The meter said they'd gone 1 mile. Then 1.2. 1.5. Almost there. "We are at the North Gate River. A woman has fallen in. She's possibly been shot. The suspect has been detained. I'm with the Sutter Springs Volunteer Fire Department. We need a water rescue crew at two miles downstream of the bridge."

The second the point nine flashed to a zero, he yelled, "That's two miles."

Isaiah nodded, his face grim. "Looking for a place to pull over, Gideon."

"Forget that. Drop me off here." He handed the phone back to Isaiah. The dispatcher was still on the line. "I'm exiting the vehicle. My brother will keep you apprised."

He didn't pay attention to her response. Isaiah would be able to keep her up to date on the situation just as well as he could. Possibly even better with his background.

Isaiah slowed down and Gideon flung open his door and hit the ground running. He made it to the edge of the river and sank down on his knees, both to be closer to the water when she passed by and so he could cry out to his Father. The river boiled and churned over the rocks and debris caused by the latest storm. It was higher than normal, creeping up on the bank. Every few seconds, a small splash hit him in his face or chest. Within a minute, the front of his shirt had large wet splotches on it. When the breeze kicked up, he shivered, his arms prickling with the chill.

He didn't move or acknowledge the discomfort. He'd withstand it all, and so much more, to have Beth safe and sound at his side. Why had he never told her he loved her?

Another drop of water smacked into him, hitting him in the eyes. He blinked and kept his gaze focused on the moving river.

"*Gott*, please. Help me find her. Please don't take her from me." It felt like a selfish prayer, but it was a cry from his heart. He became aware of the tears streaming down his face when his vision blurred. Impatient, he swiped his sleeve across his face so he wouldn't miss her.

Suddenly, a head popped above the water. Yes! It was Beth. Her hair had fallen almost completely out of its bun, the long chestnut strands dripping wet and snagging on branches. Beth's mouth opened wide. She gulped for air. Her face was completely white. Then her head disappeared under the water again. His heart pounded in his chest. He kept track of where she should be. Slipping onto his belly near the edge, he reached out his arms, praying for the grace to catch her as she floated past.

She broke free and surfaced. This time her face was looking directly at him. Their eyes met. He shifted forward. Her arms broke through and stretched toward him.

Her ice-cold fingertips grazed his. She whimpered, spreading her fingers wide to make them stretch farther. Just a couple more inches and he'd have her.

"*Cumme* on, Beth. Almost there." He scooted closer, moving his torso dangerously far out over the water.

Suddenly, the current lifted her out of his reach and carried her downstream.

"*Nee!*" Bounding to his feet, he raced down the riverbank, ignoring the branches snatching at his trousers and scratching his arms, shouting at her. "Beth! Grab onto something. Anything! A tree! A branch. I'm coming."

He jumped over a root and kept going. Where was Isaiah?

Up ahead, Beth surfaced again. She was heading toward a large oak tree, half sprawled across the riverbank. The massive tree had been mostly uprooted, no doubt by the last storm. Its roots were as tall as a full grown man. They'd left a gaping hole in the earth when they'd been yanked free.

"Beth! Grab the oak tree!"

He doubted she could hear him above the rushing of the water.

Gideon pumped his arms to move faster and prayed harder than he could remember ever praying in his life.

She plunged below the water again and swallowed a mouthful of cold liquid. River water wasn't always fresh. It was a mix of fresh water, mud, silt and sediment due to erosion, debris from the current and other unknown objects.

Beth pushed her face above the water and spat the filthy liquid from her mouth. She had swallowed so much dirty water that her lungs ached. She struggled to get a full breath. But between the force of the current pressing in on her and the debris pummeling her, plus the water surging over her head time and time again, she was failing. How long could she survive this before she drowned?

Gideon's hands had touched hers. Another two inches and he would have pulled her ashore.

Tears tracked down her face. She barely felt them. Her skin was so cold, numbing the pain in her body. Which couldn't be *gut*. Her body was one large aching bruise. She didn't think she could keep her head above the surface much longer. She was so tired. When her forehead touched the surface, she jerked upright. She hadn't realized she'd closed her eyes, or that her head had begun to droop forward. She must stay vigilant. She couldn't give in. She wanted to live. Wanted to be with Gideon.

Gideon knew where she was. She couldn't see or hear him anymore, but she had heard him as she fell into the river. And she had seen him a few minutes before. Again, her mind recalled how close rescue had been. They had touched. If only she had been a few inches closer, she might even now be out of the freezing river and wrapped in his arms. It seemed her life in the past few days had been a rash of close calls. And always, Gideon had been there for her.

It felt cruel that after all they'd gone through, this could be the end.

Her long hair wrapped around a branch. Pain burst through her skull. A moment later, her wounded arm bumped into an object. She yelped. But stopped moving. The river current continued to press in on her, but she was held tight between the thick trunk of a fallen tree and the river current.

She allowed herself to rest for a few moments, just long enough to catch her breath. When her lids dropped over her eyes again, she forced them open. She would have time to rest once she was safe. Right now, if she allowed herself to close her eyes, she would die.

And she wasn't ready to die yet.

Forcing herself into motion, she tried first to free her hair. Some of the thick strands were wrapped around the branch too tight. If she had scissors, she would have cut it. That wasn't an option she had. Grabbing hold of a section of her hair wrapped around the branch, she yanked until the hair broke free, leaving large clumps knotted around the limb. She didn't have time for vanity. It was only hair and would grow back.

She repeated the process two more times. The last bit of hair had attached itself to a slim twig. Instead of ripping the hair, she snapped the twig off at the base, leaving it entwined in her curls. She could deal with it later. Right now, she needed to get out of the water.

"Beth!"

Her heart slammed against her rib cage. She turned her head to the left and met Gideon's concerned gaze. All the color had drained from his handsome, familiar face. She saw from the determination in his deep blue eyes that he hadn't given up, even though she could tell he was scared. So was she.

But he was still too far away. Weariness clouded her mind. The urge to sleep tugged at her. She fought it, knowing it would lead to death. But what could she do against the forces of nature?

"I can't get to you," she croaked out, her voice raw.

"I know, *liebling*." She didn't have time to dwell on the fact he'd just called her darling. "I want you to climb on this tree. Get on it and hold tight. The water rescue team is on its way."

"I'll try." She wanted to tell him she loved him, just in case she wasn't strong enough, but that felt too much like she had given up. *Nee*, she would tell him when she was safe and able to stand on her own two feet to tell him all those things herself. And she would ask for forgiveness for her anger that he had chosen Miriam and then abandoned her family.

Enough. She pushed the irrelevant thoughts aside and wrapped her arms around the thick tree. Lifting her legs, she found footholds amid the branches. It took some doing, but she managed to get her torso completely free of the rushing river. Her skirts were soaked, the heavy material making her movements slow and laborious. By the time she had scrambled on top of the tree leaning across the flowing river like it was taking a bow, her hands were raw, and her legs and knees were scraped.

She found a large limb standing upright that was roughly as thick as her body. Placing her arms around the branch, she sat on the main trunk and held on. Her right bicep ached. Glancing down, she noticed a small hole in the fabric. While the rest of her dress was in tatters from the river, this rip was different. Grayson's bullet had grazed her.

"Stay there, Beth," Gideon called out to her.

"I will." Where else would she go?

Opening her eyes, she twisted her head to the left and caught his fierce gaze and allowed the warmth of his stare to ease some of her worry and fear.

A group of men surrounded him. She saw the scuba diving gear. His gaze broke from hers and he frowned at a man holding a walkie-talkie.

"—need to do a threat assessment. Can a rescue be attempted with reasonable safety?"

The man with the walkie-talkie grimaced. "Yes, sir. The victim is out of the water, sitting on an uprooted tree."

"It's not steady," another man interrupted. "The tree is likely to break free at any time."

What were they saying? They wouldn't be able to *cumme* and get to her? After all this, she refused to believe *Gott* intended for her to die now.

Isaiah and Gideon both moved to the base of the tree.

"Beth, can you inch your way toward us?" Gideon's voice had a new tremor to it. Other than that, he gave no indication of fear.

She swallowed. Her vocal cords seemed unwilling to work, so she settled on nodding her agreement. Slowly, she eased her grip on the branch and pulled her legs up on the tree trunk in order to rearrange her limbs to a kneeling position. It took some work, and a constant litany of prayer, but she started inching her way on hands and knees toward them.

"Easy," the man with the walkie-talkie called. "That tree seems to be a bit shaky."

Even as the man spoke, a shudder shook the tree. It lurched and slid six inches. The branch she held on to tilted. Beth scrambled up higher on the trunk, placing herself behind the branch rather than beside it.

"Back up! We don't want anyone caught if it goes."

Several of the men stepped away.

"I'm not leaving without Beth."

Gideon's voice cut through all discussion like a sharp blade. He muttered to his brother and Isaiah turned and jogged back to his car. She kept her gaze on Gideon. He would get her out of this. He and his brother. Gideon might have fallen for her sister's false charm once before, but even as fallible as he was, he remained the steadiest person in her life. She knew he would figure this out.

Soon, Isaiah returned, a thick rope in his hands. He tied one end around another tree, one that hadn't been damaged by the recent storms, and then Gideon moved toward her.

He tossed her the end. She caught it in her sore hands. Ignoring the pain, she clung to the rope.

"*Liebling*, you'll have to *cumme* to us. Slowly. I can't get closer to you, or the tree will roll more. It would suck you under."

She nodded. She could visualize what he was saying. If it rolled, she might get trapped under it and drown before they were able to pull her to safety. Impatience itched under her skin. If only she could stand on the huge trunk and run the distance between them.

But she couldn't. Every millimeter she moved, the unstable tree wobbled. Finally, she was less than three feet from Gideon. She was going to make it. A laugh gurgled inside, but she held it in. She was so close.

Two feet.

She'd be there in less than a minute.

She lifted her hand, and the tree began to roll.

She wouldn't make it.

SIXTEEN

Gideon could practically feel her breath on his face. Beth's shining eyes suddenly opened wide. The hope was displaced by a sudden terror.

He knew what was happening.

"It's rolling!"

No way was he letting her go.

"Beth, jump!" Gideon placed himself at the edge of the bank, as close to the tree as he dared. If he made the mistake of stepping in the water, he would either be swept away by the current or carried under the fallen tree.

Beth stood on the tree, flailed her arms like she was on a tight rope, then took a running leap at him. Her body crashed into his and they both went down in a pile of arms and sodden clothes. The tree gave one last shudder, then broke free and rolled. The branch she'd been holding on to dipped into the water. Had she remained on the tree, it would have trapped her.

There was no way she would have survived that.

He hugged her close, uncaring that there were people surrounding them or that she was drenched. His tears mingled with hers. She sobbed his name. Unable to keep his feelings from bursting out a second longer, he bent and kissed her lips. It lasted a mere second, and then they were both being pulled upright and surrounded, blankets thrown around them.

Suddenly, he remembered. "You were shot!"

The voices stilled.

"My arm." She winced. "The bullet grazed my arm. I forgot about it, but it's wonderful sore now."

"Okay, miss. An ambulance is on the way," someone said.

Her gaze flew to Gideon. They both remembered the last time she was in the hospital. "You have to get checked out. But I'll go with you. We are not leaving you on your own. Now after all that's happened."

He sat with her, side by side, waiting for the ambulance to arrive. They didn't speak. Too many people were busy around them. Her head rested against his shoulder. He kissed the top of her hair.

"I lost my *kapp*," she mourned.

"*Ja*, I know."

"It could have been so much worse."

He shuddered to think how much worse. He didn't want to imagine trying to navigate this world without her in his life. Not now that they'd found each other again. Although, he didn't know if she felt the same way he did.

What if she wanted to be friends again? Could she learn to trust him and his love for her enough to give them a chance? Would he be willing or able to accept mere friendship, when his heart wanted to shout to the world that he loved her and wanted to marry her? Could he sacrifice his dream for hers?

Glancing down at her bare head again, he decided: yes. If that was the only way he could be with her, then that would have to suffice.

He prayed that wasn't how it would be.

She had, after all, kissed him back. It had been a brief, barely there kiss. But a kiss, nonetheless.

Daisy bounded up to them, fluffy tail wagging. She sat before them with her tongue lolling.

"Aww, sweet Daisy. You were a hero today." Beth slipped her arms around the border collie and squeezed. Gideon reached out and scratched her behind her ear. The dog's tail thumped wildly on the dirt.

"Someone's happy." Isaiah plopped down on Gideon's other side. "You two doing all right? Any signs of shock?"

"Not yet. I think we'll be fine. Where's Steve?"

"Our brother-in-law insisted on handling Grayson personally. He's escorting him back to the precinct to, as he said, be booked and begin the next phase of the rest of his life behind bars."

"Can't say I'm sorry."

"Me neither."

The ambulance arrived, pulling along the edge of the road. Two paramedics left the vehicle and made their way over to Gideon and Beth. "See to her first. She's been shot in the arm."

He didn't move away any farther than he had to when they began checking her vital signs. "We should get you to the hospital to get you checked out."

"I'll go, but he has to *cumme*, too." Beth pointed an imperious finger at Gideon. He grinned, loving the way she got her sass back. He had feared he'd never see this side of her again.

The paramedics sighed and exchanged glances. "Not in the ambulance. He can follow and meet you at the hospital."

"I'll take him," Isaiah said, standing. "Don't worry, Beth. We'll be right behind you."

The last thing Gideon wanted was to be parted from her

right now, but he knew it wasn't his choice to make. So, when she gave him a somewhat panicked look, he smiled.

"With the way Isaiah drives, we might actually beat you to the hospital."

Beth rolled her eyes but didn't argue with the paramedics. Had Grayson not been on the way to the police station, it would not have been easy to convince her. However, the danger had been eliminated. Life could resume.

Although, it would never again be the life she had lived prior to Tuesday morning. He mourned the loss of that part of her life. Her father had been an innocent man who trusted the wrong people and paid with his life.

Where would she go? She probably wouldn't want to live in her *haus*, not after all that had happened. While the structure hadn't been irreparably damaged by the fire, it was still too close to the place where she'd watched her father die right before Grayson attacked her for the first time.

If they were to get married…

He shook his head and followed Isaiah to his car. Whistling for Daisy, he held the back door open for the canine, who happily hopped up on the back seat. He couldn't let himself think of marrying Beth yet. He still needed to see what she felt about him.

His gut twisted inside him. He would know soon enough. Fortunately, they were close enough to home that the ambulance headed to Sutter Springs Hospital. Even if the ambulance got too far ahead of them, they'd still know the way there.

Isaiah dropped him off at the front of the hospital. Gideon strolled in and approached the front desk. The woman behind it saw him and her eyes widened behind the round rims of her glasses. He glanced down. His shirt was torn, and blood stained it. He had been so intent on rescuing Beth that he hadn't noticed the branches ripping at his flesh until after she was in his arms, safe.

"A woman was brought in by ambulance. Elizabeth Troyer."

The lady gave him a suspicious glance, then switched to her monitor. "Yes, she's in the emergency room, cell four. Are you Gideon Bender?"

"I am." He nodded.

"I have directions to send you back as soon as you arrive."

He would see Beth soon. He followed the security guard that the receptionist paged through the swinging doors and then to the curtained off cell. When he went in, Beth was waiting for him. She was scratched, bruised, the sleeve of her dress was ripped and a bandage covered her wound.

He'd never seen anyone more beautiful.

She held out her arms, and he went into them like he was coming home. "I thought I'd lost you when I saw you go over the ledge."

She sniffed. "To be honest, I thought you had lost me, too. Gideon, the water…it was so fast. I couldn't keep my head above the water. It terrified me. It will be a long time before I willingly go swimming in that river."

He smiled at her reference to some of their childhood antics, swimming in the river and catching fish. It had been an easier time back then. The rules had been simple, and it was before Miriam had *cumme* between them.

"We'll take it little by little. Maybe one day, you'll agree to go fishing again. Has the doctor been in to see you?"

She nodded. "You just missed him. I might feel a bit waterlogged and bruised, but I'm *gut*. The nurse will be in soon with my discharge papers."

"That's quick. I would have expected you to wait another hour."

"*Ja*. Me, too. He said it's been a slow day."

He took a deep breath. He hadn't *cumme* to talk about fishing or the wait time at the hospital. He'd promised himself that he would tell her how he felt. His heart pounded so hard that it almost hurt. Fear? Excitement? Probably a mix of both. Gideon had gotten so *gut* at hiding his emotions and keeping himself distant.

This was a new challenge. One he didn't dare fail.

He backed up enough to see her face. Her hair had dried, but still hung about her shoulders. It was gorgeous, but out of respect for her he trained his gaze on her face. Only her husband should see her hair unbound like that, but she had no control over the events of the day.

"What's wrong, Gideon?" Her gaze swept over his face. "You look upset."

"I'm not upset. Not exactly. But I do need to tell you something and I don't know how you'll take it."

She stiffened in his arms. "Just tell me."

He smiled. "You are always saying that to me."

When she didn't smile back, he pressed on. "I know you might not feel the same. You might want to remain friends. And if that is what you want, let me know. But I wanted you to know I love you, Beth Troyer. More than I ever loved your sister. I love you, and I don't want to go back to a life without you."

Beth stopped breathing and stared at him. She couldn't have heard him right. Gideon loved Miriam, not her. Didn't he? Then she recalled the way he had stood on the shore and reached out to her. He had gotten so close to the rushing water. Close enough that if he had gone just an inch or two more, he could have gone into the water, too, and drowned.

Could she allow herself to love him back?

And what about what had happened when Miriam had left him? *Nee,* she had forgiven him that, and she knew that Miriam had been more at fault.

And so had she. For Gideon had never known that Beth had seen him as more than a friend. But how could he go from friendship to love in just a few days?

A new memory surfaced in her mind. How could she have forgotten the kiss he'd given her just a couple of hours ago? At the time, she had assumed it was just a kiss of relief. After all, they'd come so close to dying. She had been shot and then fell into the river. Of course, his relief would show itself in such an exuberant gesture. She also remembered her regret not telling him how she felt. But now that the danger had passed, her certainty that she wanted to share her feelings had dwindled. The doubts had crowded in, pushing the hope aside.

How could she trust him? All her life, she had been compared to her beautiful older sister. She had watched as gorgeous Miriam had flirted her way into the hearts of one young man after another. Miriam hadn't cared whose heart she broke. And none of the men seemed to cotton on to what she was doing. Not even Gideon, as brilliant as he was, had seen her flirtation for the selfish power play that it was.

What would happen if her sister returned? She had no proof that her older sister had changed her ways in the past two years. What if she gave her heart to him, and Miriam interfered? Could she trust that Gideon wouldn't fall prey to her again?

Then she knew it wasn't about Gideon at all. It was about herself. Beth loved the man standing so hopefully in front of her. She always had loved him but had convinced herself that they were only friends. And could only ever be friends. Then her sister had proven her correct.

Now he stood here and offered her his heart. She was afraid to accept it. Afraid that one day, Gideon would wake up and discover that Beth wasn't who he wanted after all.

She would never be one of those dainty girls who sat and sewed all day. She loved the outdoors and loved taking part in all the heavy lifting and physical chores that her father had taught her to do. She would always enjoy racing down the road or throwing a football with her friends.

"I love you, too, Gideon."

He started to smile, and she hurried to finish.

"I love you, but I don't know if I can be with you. So much has happened. I have to deal with everything that has happened, including the loss of my home, because I can never go back there."

The smile had faded from his face. "So, what do we do?"

"I need time," she whispered. "And so do you."

That was possibly the most difficult phrase she had ever said in her life. Her heart screamed at her to take it back. To say she didn't need any time. That she knew what she wanted now. But she couldn't do that. It wouldn't be fair to either one of them. Before she accepted all that he offered, she had to be sure that she could live up to it. Gideon was a very special man. He deserved a woman who could be by his side at all times.

A woman who would trust him no matter what. Hopefully, she would end up being that woman. But she had to step back and find out first.

"Time for what?" His face was blank, but she could read him. She knew she had hurt him, and she hadn't wanted that.

"Gideon, last week if we'd met at a church function, we wouldn't have talked. Not at all. This week, my father was murdered, and I was under constant attack. Emotions were running high. I need time to figure out what is real."

She drew a deep breath. "I loved you when I was twenty."

His eyes grew wide. "I had no idea."

"*Ja*, I know you didn't. I knew the moment she saw it, my sister would go after you. Just to prove she could. Which she did. And you fell for it, as others have, too. I never loved anyone else but you."

"Am I why you never married?" So much anguish was in his voice.

She nodded.

"Then why not accept me now?"

"Because I need you to be sure this is what you really want. And I need to be sure, too."

Leaning close, she kissed his cheek. "Goodbye, Gideon. Hopefully, I will see you soon. Don't bother coming by my *haus*. I won't be there. That *haus* is too full of bad memories."

"Where will you be?"

She shrugged. "Probably with my family in Pennsylvania. But I'll *cumme* back. If for no other reason than to tell you what I've decided. I won't leave you wondering."

"Look, do you have money to take you where you need to go?"

She shook her head. He took out his wallet and pulled out a few bills. She started to protest.

Gideon narrowed his eyes and glared. "You need money, ain't so? This is the Amish way. We help each other out. Always. You can pay me back when you return."

The words *if you return to me* hung between them. She knew he struggled with leaving her. He paled. The devastated expression on his face hurt her. She nearly changed her mind. She couldn't. If they had any kind of future, she had to be strong. If he still loved her when she returned, and if she could work through her doubts, then maybe there would be a happy ending for them.

Gideon opened his mouth, then shut it, swallowing. He leaned forward and gently kissed her forehead. She couldn't speak over the lump in her throat.

He turned and walked out of the cubicle, casting one last glance over his shoulder, his eyes damp.

Beth listened to his steps fade away. Had she done the right thing? Dropping her head into her hands, she let the tears fall for a moment.

Then she lifted her head and straightened her shoulders. She had plans to make. She couldn't walk to LaMar Pond. That was at least a two-and-a-half-hour drive. Nor could she remain in the hospital. Her discharge papers would arrive at any second.

As if reading her mind, the nurse entered with a clipboard. "You're all good to go, honey. I just need to go over these forms and get your signature."

She nodded and listened to the nurse explain what was in the papers. The words swam in front of her eyes. She blinked and accepted the pen the woman handed to her. Quickly, she signed her name.

"You're all set."

"Wait." Beth stopped her from exiting. "I need to call for a ride."

The nurse smiled. "Come out to the front desk with me. We'll call for you."

Biting her lip, she tried to decide who to call. She didn't have a list of Amish drivers memorized. What could she do? She tapped her fingers against her chin while she thought.

Susannah's! The quilt shop was five miles away, so she couldn't walk it. Even without all the bruises, she wouldn't attempt it. But if she got a taxi to the quilt shop, maybe she'd be able to ask Susanna and her mother for help finding a driver to take her to her family in Pennsylvania. It was the only option she had at the moment.

Ten minutes later, Beth thanked the receptionist and walked out of the hospital and got into the back seat of the taxi waiting for her. She told the driver to take her to Susanna's quilt shop. "Sure can." He set the meter and pulled away from the hospital.

She signed and let her head fall against the window. Closing her eyes, she attempted to shut out the world for a few minutes.

"We're here."

Startled, she sat up. That was fast. She exited the vehicle and paid the driver. *"Denke."*

Her feet crunched across the gravel on the shoulder of the road. She skirted the grassy area and made her way to the slim walkway. At the door, she paused. Once she went in, she would have to follow through and find a driver. She wouldn't ask Susanna's family for shelter. They'd give it, she had no doubt, but she needed to follow through on her decision. Pressing her lips tightly together, she opened the door and entered.

Susanna's mother glanced up from behind the counter.

"Beth!" She stood and made her way across the room. "How are you?"

"Gut." She smiled at her former friend's mother. "I need to hire a driver to bring me to visit my family in Pennsylvania. Do you have a list of drivers handy?"

If the older woman thought it odd that Beth appeared without a *kapp* and her dress in tatters, she gave no sign of it.

"There's a list next to the phone in the back room." The woman pointed her to the room. She flipped through the names. The first two she tried were already busy. She dialed the third number. While she waited for the phone to be picked up, her old friend approached her.

"Susanna!" she greeted her. "I didn't think you were here."

"*Ja*, I just got home. Mamm said your *kapp* was missing." She handed her a fresh white *kapp*, then allowed her gaze to peer at the poor condition of Beth's dress. "I don't think my shoes will fit you, but I may have an old dress of my sister's that you can wear."

"*Denke!*" Beth whispered gratefully. A clean dress would be wonderful *gut*. Before she could say more, someone on the other end of the line picked up.

"Hello?" a voice on the phone answered.

"Tony Starns?"

"This is him."

"I'm looking for a driver to take me to LaMar Pond, Pennsylvania." While he checked his schedule, she glanced out the shop window.

Gideon walked past, shoulders hunched in sorrow. She'd assumed he'd already left. She ducked down so he wouldn't see her and watched as he got into Isaiah's car. She stilled the impulse to run after him. She couldn't do that. She had been truthful. Before she committed herself to Gideon, she had to sort through everything.

If *Gott* willed it, she'd be back soon to take her place at his side.

In her ear, she heard Tony say he was free. Tearing her gaze away from where she'd seen Gideon, she made plans to go to Pennsylvania, feeling as if a hole had opened up inside her heart.

SEVENTEEN

He hadn't seen or heard from Beth in exactly two weeks. It was the longest fourteen days in his memory. Each morning, he'd wake up and he'd spend fifteen minutes thinking about her and wondering where she could have gone. Last week, he'd been out and had taken the buggy on the "scenic way home," as Micah would have said, deliberately driving out of his way to go past the Troyer property.

He knew she wouldn't be there. Of course, she wouldn't. Between her *daed*'s murder and the destruction to both the barn and the *haus*, it would be unwise and too painful for Beth to stay there alone. And she was stubborn enough that he knew she wouldn't *cumme* to him until she was ready.

He had to respect that. Her strong spirit was one of the parts of her he loved most.

All he could do was love her from afar and hold her up in prayer daily. He held a constant vigil in his heart for her. And he had faith. One day, *Gott* willing, his Beth would return. Gideon had no choice but to accept that. His family grew concerned. He caught the looks they threw his way. He hated worrying them, but there was nothing he could do.

At least he knew Beth wasn't alone. She was with relatives while she came to terms with all that had occurred.

He had no address for them, though, so had no choice but to wait and pray.

Making his way to the shop, he idly glanced up at the sky and analyzed the clouds. They were wispy, drifting lazily across the blue background of the sky. "Cirrus clouds. Not many of them. Lots of space between them. At least 6,000 meters above us. Looks like a beautiful day."

It would be a lovely day to go for a walk. But only with Beth. He didn't feel like enjoying nature without knowing how she was faring.

He hadn't reached the shop when two familiar vehicles pulled in, one after the other. He stopped walking. No sense going into the shop when his brothers were here to see him. He'd been expecting them to drop by. Honestly, it amazed him that it had taken them fourteen long days before they decided to corner him. A smile tugged at the corners of his lips.

Micah hopped out of the first vehicle. Gideon raised his eyebrows when Zeke climbed out of the passenger seat. Isaiah slammed his car door and joined the other two. The three men ambled over to Gideon.

"We're here to stage an intervention," Isaiah announced.

"I can see that." Gideon looked beyond them to make sure they were alone. "I'm surprised you didn't bring Joss along with you."

Micah grinned, the corners of his eyes crinkling. "Our little sister isn't feeling so well this morning."

All humor fled from Gideon. "Why are you bothering with me? Is she going to be okay? Has Steve taken her to the doctor?"

Both Isaiah and Micah laughed. Zeke grew a little red around his ears. What—? Oh. Understanding dawned. In many districts, some topics were not spoken of outside the family. Such as pregnancy. Indeed, many *kinder* were kept in the dark about new siblings until the mother was in labor. No wonder Zeke looked embarrassed. Micah and Isaiah had no such issues since both lived in the *Englisch* world where their wives' pregnancies had been openly celebrated.

"So, little Christina and Tim will have a new sister or brother soon, ain't so?"

Two of the other men nodded. Zeke merely grinned and shrugged.

"That's *gut*. You're sure she's fine, *ja*?"

Isaiah gave him a calm down gesture. "Relax, little bro. Yes. She's fine. She's happy and excited about the baby, just tired. Steve's over the moon."

He was going to be an *oncle* again. He sighed. He loved his nieces and nephews. But he was ready to be a husband and a *daed*.

"I hear that sigh," Micah growled. "That's why we're here. You are not happy, Gid. And we know why."

That was fair. He shrugged. What they said was true, but he was powerless to change his situation at the moment. Once Beth returned, however, he planned on asking her to marry him as soon as he could spit the words out of his mouth. He knew they would probably wait to get married until fall. That's when Amish weddings typically happened. But he could wait as long as necessary if he knew she was his.

He was getting ahead of himself. She might reject him, still.

"Dude, you told us when we were being stupid about our wives. We don't want to see you make the same mistakes," Isaiah said.

"I wasn't stupid," Zeke muttered. "I was in the hospital healing from a gunshot wound."

Isaiah nudged him with his elbow, hard. The brothers all laughed. The laughter died quickly, though, and the other three faced him. Gideon refused to get emotional. He cleared his throat twice.

"*Denke*. It means the world to me that you want to help me. But I'm not sure there's anything you can do."

Micah stepped forward. "We know you love her. Is she the one who broke your heart?"

Gideon winced. He hadn't told his brothers what had happened with Miriam. "*Nee*. Not her. I had been walking out with someone else."

He couldn't tell them everything. It felt like a betrayal to Beth to expose her and her family like that.

"Then Beth—"

He turned to Zeke. "Beth is the best friend I've ever had. I failed her and we didn't talk for two years. But *ja*, I love her."

"You… you should tell her." Zeke's quiet voice shut them all down. Zeke had been married before, and his wife had died a violent death after betraying him. He was happy now, and Molly had brought light and joy back into his life.

"I have told her."

They stared at him. It was almost funny.

"You have?" Micah shook his head. "Then why are we having this conversation?"

Gideon did laugh, a rusty bark of sound. "Because she needs time to sort out everything that happened. Her *daed* dying. Her sister wrote that she was returning, who knows when. Someone almost killed her. She knows how I feel. If it's *Gott*'s plan, she will *cumme* back to me. I will be here waiting for her."

"What if she doesn't *cumme* back?"

He smiled at Zeke. "Then I will still be here, helping *Daed* and *Mamm*."

As far as he was concerned, that was the end of it.

"Gideon…"

He held in a sigh and looked at Micah.

"I would never presume to tell you that you could find someone else to love. We all know that isn't the case. But we are all here for you. No matter what."

He nodded, unable to speak for a moment.

"What he said," Isaiah echoed.

"*Denke.* I appreciate it. I don't know if I would ever find anyone who understands me the way she does. Or who accepts me and doesn't expect me to change what I can't change."

"You mean that you're a genius." Isaiah nodded as if it all made sense. Gideon stared around the circle of brothers surrounding him. Not a one of them seemed surprised by the statement.

"We've always known your mind worked a little different," Zeke said, his voice soft. "But it didn't matter. That was how *Gott* made you."

Gideon shook his head. All these years he'd made light of it. Hidden it, in a way. And his family knew the entire time and accepted him. How had he missed it?

"Well, we're here. We might as well see if *Mamm* has some cinnamon rolls made," Micah stated.

"She does."

Laughing, the brothers returned to the haus.

Gideon was still thinking about the conversation two hours later when he hitched up his mare and drove the buggy into town. He didn't see Miriam until he was almost trodding on her feet. She'd placed herself directly in his path. He halted so fast he almost tripped. He had to in order to avoid running over her.

And just like that, he knew she hadn't changed at all in

the past two years. Same pale blonde hair, although now she wore it long instead of up under an Amish *kapp*. Same big blue eyes that always seemed so helpless. He used to dream about those eyes. Now, the helpless act annoyed him.

No. She hadn't changed at all. But he had. Now when he looked at Miriam, he couldn't help but compare her to Beth. And found her wanting.

Whereas Miriam had left the moment things got a little dull, Beth stood strong when things got hard. Beth was a woman who one could depend on, one who wouldn't give in to whims or flights of fancy.

"Miriam." He greeted her. He wouldn't lie and say it was *gut* to see her. She had come so close to ruining his life before. He also knew how much she had hurt Beth with her selfishness. No, he would not say he was happy to see her. However, he wouldn't be rude to her. Obviously, she had something she needed to say since she had put herself right in front of him. He would let her say it, and then he would go on his way.

"Gideon." She gave him a bright smile. The smile faded when he didn't respond in kind. "I've been looking for you."

"You found me."

"Yes. I stopped by your shop. Your father said you were coming to the lumber yard. So, I drove out here and waited for you." She gestured to her car. It was obviously new, spotless. And completely removed from the plain way of life. Anyone seeing her would never guess she was once Amish.

"What did you need to see me about?"

He needed to get home and finish a project. He didn't have time for her games. Not now. Not ever again.

"Well, I wanted to apologize."

His eyes widened. He'd never imagined he'd hear those words from her. "What are you apologizing for?"

She flushed. "Look, I knew you were planning on proposing to me. I'd led you on, making you think I wanted the same thing."

"You didn't, though, did you? You just wanted me because you knew your sister and I had a strong friendship."

Her lips turned down at the corners. Clearly, she didn't want him to know everything. "Fine. Yes, I saw that and got jealous. She seemed to have it all. But I thought I was better. Prettier. I hurt her. And I hurt you. I regret it now. So, I wanted to say I was sorry."

He stared into her eyes. Was she truly sorry? Only *Gott* knew that. He wouldn't deny forgiveness. That wasn't who he was. However, that didn't mean he accepted what she had done.

"I forgive you, Miriam. But you owe a bigger apology to your sister. I expect you owe her a lifetime of apologies."

Her sister. He winced. Did she know about her father?

Her face paled slightly. "I know. I went by my old house before coming to find you. I was shocked to see it gone. I knew my *daed* was dead. I still have a couple of friends in Sutter Springs. Not Amish friends. One of them called me last week to tell me that my father had died. I've been living in New York. I took a leave from my job and came as soon as I could. I planned on apologizing. I'd like to be friends again. With my sister. And with you. But I couldn't find her."

He shook his head. "*Nee*. I choose to forgive you. But I don't want you in my life. Not anymore. If Beth wants you in hers, I won't object. But that's it. I wish you well."

She stepped back as if shocked. Swallowed. "I deserve that. Can you tell me where she is?"

Despite what she'd done, he knew he couldn't keep her away from her family. "She's with relatives in Pennsylvania."

She nodded. "I know where. Look, I'll make it right with her."

"See that you do."

He walked away from her, knowing he'd done all he could. Miriam was like an insidious disease. She apologized, and she was clearly not content with her life. But she'd been a parasite for so long, he couldn't trust that she had changed. Not yet. And he would never again put Miriam ahead of Beth. He'd made that mistake once and had lost the best friend he'd ever had. Now he had fallen in love with Beth. And whether or not she chose to reciprocate, he would never betray her.

"You don't need to pull into the driveway," Beth said, turning away from the window and handing her driver the money she owed him. Maybe she was being ridiculous, but she didn't want to announce her presence to the family. If she could walk to the carpentry shop and speak with Gideon alone, she would prefer to do it that way. The young man behind the wheel accepted the bills, frowning.

"Will you need me to wait for you? Or I can come back in a while. I'm free this afternoon."

She hesitated, turning her head toward Gideon's *haus*. She hadn't told him she was stopping by. If it was an awkward time for him, or if he had changed his mind…

Nee. She knew Gideon better than that. He was faithful. He'd told her he loved her three weeks ago. Now it was time that she showed him she was ready and able to return his feelings and move on with their future.

"Denke," she said, smiling at the driver. "I'm sure it won't be necessary, but if it is, I can call from my friend's office."

He shrugged. "Whatever. If that's the way you want to do it."

She squared her shoulders, then threw open the door and stepped out. She let the door shut gently behind her and stepped off the road and onto the gravel driveway. Small puffs of dust rose with every step. It had been nine days since the last rain and the ground was dry. Once she would have ignored the sight of the dirt rising and coating her boots. That was before she'd spent days without her vision. Now, seeing the particles floating in the air, she again thanked *Gott* for His providence. She had *cumme* so close to dying, to never being able to appreciate such simple things again.

She wouldn't take any of it for granted.

The shop loomed ahead of her. She quickened her step, her pulse jumping. Soon. Very soon, she'd see Gideon again.

The door was partially open. It was a warm day but there was a light breeze. As she drew near, she heard the scraping and pounding of someone hard at work. Swallowing hard, she edged closer to the door. Pulling it wider so she could slip through, she paused in the entryway.

Gideon stood next to the table. He hadn't noticed her yet. She caught her breath, watching him narrow his eyes and place a pencil mark on the two-by-four lying on the table. He stood back and ran his gaze over the length of the board again. Then he nodded, satisfied.

It never failed to amaze her how he could measure something with his eyes. Sure enough, he reached out and pulled the saw to him and began cutting the length without bothering with a tape measure.

It would be a perfect measurement, she knew. Gideon had a gift.

He set the saw back on the table. She shifted her stance

and he stilled. Then he whirled to face her, his mouth dropping open.

"Beth!"

"Gideon." She moved farther into the room. All the words she had planned so carefully to say died in her throat. Her eyes met his. She had to blink to clear the moisture blurring her view of this brave, bright man who'd once broken her heart, then nearly died to save her life and make it whole again.

"I hoped you'd *cumme* soon," he murmured.

Searching his face for a hint of bitterness or anger, she found none. Still, the lingering signs of sorrow stamped on his features pierced her heart. She had caused that. Because she refused to trust and accept the gift *Gott* had given them.

"I'm sorry I stayed away so long," she blurted. "I regretted walking away almost immediately, but I couldn't figure out what else to do."

He nodded. "*Ja*. I understand."

That didn't surprise her at all. When he stretched out a hand, she reached out and grabbed hold like it was a lifeline.

"There's more I need to tell you." She swallowed. "I'd called the Sutter Springs Police Department from Pennsylvania so they'd know where I was, in case there was any more news. Steve came to see me a couple of days ago."

"He did? What did he say?"

"Remember how we had wondered why Lonnie Nelson had hidden the drugs at my *haus*? It turns out he had stolen them from Grayson, who had been stealing from the hospital lab. When he came up short, Grayson figured it out. He followed Lonnie to my *haus*. When he saw my *daed* pay Lonnie, he thought my *daed* was helping Lonnie sell his drugs. He wasn't. The police believe he was paying for the work he'd done on our roof."

Gideon shook his head sadly. "Your *daed* truly was a victim of circumstances."

"He was. He was a *gut* and honest man. I will miss him."

A shadow crossed his face. "I have some news to tell you, as well," he said,

Quirking an eyebrow at him, she waited.

He sighed. "Your sister came to see me."

"Did she?"

There was no censure in the word. Never again would Miriam *cumme* between them.

He winced. "*Ja.* She wanted to apologize for hurting me. And for hurting you."

She'd already told him about her sister's transgressions against her. What he didn't know was that Beth had talked with her sister two days after Gideon had. It had surprised her that her sister had apologized to Gideon. Miriam had never wanted to appear anything more than perfect. In her whole life, she couldn't remember Miriam ever accepting responsibility for her mistakes. Until now.

"*Ja.* I know." She smiled when his eyes bulged. "She found me in Pennsylvania and told me she'd talked with you. But she was very vague about the conversation. What did you say to her?"

The corner of his mouth tugged upward. He shrugged. "I told her I forgive her, but she needed to apologize to you more than she did to me. Doesn't mean I want her in my life. She seemed very unhappy."

"Well, she apologized, but I'm not sure how sincere she is. I have her address and contact information. She is staying in New York for now. She is planning on visiting regularly from now on. I don't think she knows if she wants to stay *Englisch* or return to the Amish life. Although I can't see her returning to our life permanently, she doesn't seem happy. I will forgive her. But I don't think we'll ever have a close bond. At least not yet."

Beth couldn't promise that she would ever want a deeper relationship with her wayward sister. Like Gideon, forgiving her sister didn't mean she trusted her. Miriam had been a toxic presence in her life for far too long, despite being family. She'd nearly destroyed her whole family to satisfy her own ego. It was a hard thing to move beyond.

Gideon took a step closer and rubbed the back of his left hand down her cheek. Then he reached out and wrapped his fingers around her hand. She shivered.

"I also told her," Gideon whispered, "that I was wonderful happy she and I didn't get married. I thought I was in love with your sister. But it wasn't the *gut*, healthy love I feel for you. I want more than that shallow relationship. It had been very one-sided. Instead, I want to marry a woman who will be my partner. One who will accept me, and not be irritated if I do something a little different."

And Miriam would have done that. Every time Gideon did something that showed his superior intellect, she would have been annoyed at him. She liked having the spotlight all on her.

Suddenly, Beth's mind caught up with her ears.

Marry. Wife. She stopped breathing.

"Gideon," she gasped. "Are you—"

She couldn't say it. What if she was wrong and he wasn't proposing? Was it too soon?

He laughed. "Yes, Beth. I am asking you to marry me. Although apparently, I'm not doing it well. I need to change that."

She choked back a soggy laugh, rubbing her free hand across her eyes. "Then please, continue."

He took her other hand. "I know we've only been back

together for a short time. And I know I let you down. But you've been my dearest friend for so many years. I was distracted for a minute, but I see clearly now. You are the love of my life. The one person I never have to pretend with. I want to marry you, raise a family with you. When I'm old, I want to sit next to you in the chairs *Daed* and I made on the porch and laugh about all the adventures we've had over the years."

"That sounds lovely." More than lovely. He had put into words the dream she had held in her own heart.

"So, is that an acceptance?"

She nodded slowly, joy simmering and humming in her blood. "*Ja.* I will marry you."

He flashed her a quick grin, then leaned closer. Instinctively, she rose up and met his lips halfway. The kiss was everything she'd dreamed it would be.

Footsteps crunched on the gravel outside the door. They broke apart as his father, Nathan, entered the shop. He paused, those wise blue eyes shifting between the two of them. Suddenly, a wide grin spread across his face.

"*Welkum* to the family, Beth."

He didn't miss much. She burst out laughing. The future had never looked so bright.

EPILOGUE

In a few hours, he would be a married man and no longer alone.

Gideon bounded down the steps and jogged out to the barn. His *daed* would be joining him soon. Normally, Gideon waited until *Daed* was ready and they started the morning chores together. On this day, however, energy crackled and surged through his veins like he had chugged a gallon of coffee before breakfast. He'd been so amped up, *Mamm* shook her head and pointed to the back door.

"Go. Before you break something."

He hadn't argued but strode to her side and pressed a noisy kiss to her cheek, then grabbed his hat and departed through the back door while she was still laughing. Grinning, he breathed in the cool morning air. There was a bite to the chill, suggesting the possibility of some snow later. He didn't care. Snow, rain or sunshine… It didn't matter.

"This is the day which the Lord hath made; we will rejoice and be glad in it." The words from Psalm 118:24 spilled from his mouth. And indeed, his heart was light, and joy swelled inside. Regardless of the weather, today was a *gut* day.

And soon, his best friend would become his wife. After Gideon had believed that he'd wind up alone, *Gott* had shown him a different plan. His gratitude was boundless. Humming a nameless tune, he hooked the milking stool with his foot and yanked it toward himself. Setting it beside the cow, he lowered himself onto it and positioned the pail. Before he began to milk the cow, Gideon eyed the distance between the pail and the cow and mentally measuring how far he could move the bucket and still have the spray of milk hit its target. He resisted the temptation to put his theory to the test, knowing *Daed* would not appreciate it if any of the milk were spilled and wasted.

In a few hours, the one person who truly appreciated his mind would be his wife. Although, he wouldn't want to aggravate her any more than he would his father. Still, the fact that she knew him so well and continued to love him sent a wave of contentment flooding through the deepest part of his soul.

Boots tromping through the barn cut into his musings. Lifting his head, Gideon spied his father and Isaiah approaching him. A wide grin split his face. He stood from the stool and removed his gloves.

"Isaiah! I didn't expect you to *cumme* so early! Is your family here?"

Isaiah shook his head. "Nah. Addie will arrive in time for the wedding. She was up with Chloe half the night. I think she's starting to teethe."

Gideon's eyebrows inched up his forehead. "That early? She's barely five-months-old."

He'd read teething started around six months.

"What can I say? My daughter's precocious." Isaiah's words were joking, but his tone was reverent. Like Gideon, Isaiah had assumed he would never be blessed with the love of a good woman or a family. Now he had Addie and two *kinder* of his own. "Anyway, she'll arrive before the wedding."

With Isaiah to assist, the morning chores were completed in a fraction of the time. Gideon couldn't stop grinning. Or looking at the clock. Micah arrived with his family while they were cleaning up after breakfast.

"Everything ready to go?" He handed his sleeping son over to Edith, who took her toddler grandson in her arms and kissed his forehead, a serene smile on her face. She swayed gently. Gideon couldn't help but think his *mamm* was beautiful when she held one of the babies. And there were so many of them now.

Steve and Joss had three *kinder*. The baby, a little girl named Meghan, was asleep. He could hear Christina chattering in the other room. Timmy was quieter, but he was a handful now that he was walking. Micah and Lissa had ten-year-old Shelby, who was constantly shadowed by their son Ben and Addie and Isaiah's Ollie. Gideon was fairly certain, based on how protective Micah had been acting lately, they'd be adding a third *boppli* come spring, but one didn't speak of such things. Zeke and Molly's twins, Zediciah and Deborah, were huddled together, speaking to each other in twin speak. His *mamm* told him he and Joss used to do the same thing. Zeke and Molly's baby Emma was seven months-old.

One day, he and Beth would add to the growing numbers, if *Gott* willed it. He would be content with whatever they had. Beth was the greatest blessing of his life. Glancing at the clock, Gideon excused himself to get ready. Since it was his wedding day, he added a bow tie to his crisp white shirt before donning a dark vest and pulling it closed with a hook and eye.

Then he joined the family in the kitchen.

"We'd best be going," *Daed* announced. "It won't be much of a wedding without a groom and his *newehockers*."

Gideon and Isaiah glanced at each other and rolled their eyes.

"Since the wedding will be at Zeke's place, all my *newehockers* are probably already there."

Only baptized Amish were allowed to stand up with the bride and groom, which meant that Zeke was the only brother who could perform the office for Gideon. The others had all helped, though. The benches used for church were all set up in Zeke's barn. They were placed so the men would sit on one side and the women on the other, facing each other. A large tent had been erected outside to provide shade over the bleachers that had been brought in. That was where the non-Amish guests would sit. Which would include most of his brothers and his sister and their families.

But at least they would be there.

After the ceremony, they would enjoy the meal provided by the women of the community.

Micah and Isaiah had agreed to chauffeur them to Zeke's *haus*. Gideon would never remember the short journey from his parents' *haus* to the wedding. But he would also never forget his first sight of Beth. She was wearing a deep blue dress for her wedding. He knew it was a dress she had made herself and that she'd save it for church Sundays. Her cheeks were flushed, making her brown eyes sparkle.

He had never seen anything as lovely as his Beth.

She was Elizabeth Bender. Mrs. Gideon Bender. A wife to the man who set her pulse racing and made her laugh so hard that her sides ached. Beth's cheeks ached from smiling. Finally, she had married the man she loved. For so long,

Miriam's betrayal had cast a shadow over her, squelching an ambition to aspire for more than a spinster's existence.

Miriam hadn't come to the wedding. Beth had invited her erstwhile sister, but she admitted to herself that she wasn't upset by her sister's absence. She didn't need the stress her sibling's presence always caused.

On this most special of days, she was able to focus on her beloved husband. His family had swarmed about them after the meal, congratulating them. The Benders were a loud bunch.

Gideon clearly had tight bonds with his three brothers, his sister and their spouses. It touched her heart to witness their close-knit relationship. When Edith hugged her and called her "my new daughter," Beth's eyes overflowed.

She had a family again.

Normally, the wedding would have taken place at the bride's home. That hadn't been possible. Even if the *haus* wasn't a shambles, Beth refused to spend another night alone on the property where her *daed* had been gunned down. Instead, she had put the property up for sale and moved in with a friend for a short time. Now that she and Gideon were married, they would make their home with his parents. Eventually, Gideon would take over his father's business and Edith and Nathan would move into the *dawdi haus*, leaving Gideon and Beth and any *kinder* the larger *haus*. They weren't in any hurry, though. That big *haus* had plenty of room for the four of them. And once *kinder* came, it would be wonderful *gut* to have Edith and Nathan there. *Grootouders* were such a blessing!

"Are you finished, Beth?" Gideon said in her ear.

She glanced down at her plate, still half full. The dinner Beth's sisters-in-law and Edith had put together was scrumptious. The chicken, stuffing and homemade noodles were perfect. Together with the biscuits, pepper slaw and Molly's spiced hot apple slices, the entire meal was mouth-watering. The trouble was her stomach was fluttery so she could only take a few bites. She'd be hungry later.

"*Ja*. I can't eat anymore."

He flashed that crooked grin her way. Her breath hitched in her throat. "I'll feed you later if you get hungry, say? Why don't we let some others *cumme* eat?"

Nodding, she accepted the warm hand he held out to assist her and rose from her seat. There were only so many seats at an Amish wedding. The guest list had been large, meaning the guests would eat in shifts. Of course, the bride and groom, and their *newehockers*, were among the first to eat. Or in her case, try to eat.

Moving alongside Gideon, they visited with the friends and family spread throughout the *haus* and outside. Chatting and laughing, joy bubbled up inside. Gratitude and love filled her, spilling over.

The guests started leaving late in the afternoon. Gideon and Beth waved them off as they climbed up into their buggies and started off.

"I'll take you back to *Mamm* and *Daed*'s whenever you're ready to go," Micah told them.

They would stay at his parents' *haus* and in the morning their new life would begin by returning to Zeke's *haus* to help clean up from the wedding. She couldn't think of a better way.

Beth yawned and stretched before wrapping her arms around his right arm and leaning her head against his shoulder. He leaned over and kissed the top of her head. She imagined she felt the warmth of the gentle kiss through her *kapp* and sighed, content.

"*Ja*, I'm ready to go now," she assured her new husband. "It's been a wonderful *gut* day."

Micah nodded. "I'll go get the car. Back in a minute."

Together, they watched him stride away.

"Beth?"

She leaned her head back and peered into his beloved face. "*Ja?*"

"I'm wonderful glad you're my wife now. And I have thanked *Gott* every day since you told me you loved me for opening my eyes."

She knew what he referred to. Miriam. He was letting her know he'd closed the door on the past and would never look back.

She winked at him. "I'm glad you opened your eyes, too, Gideon. You were blind too long."

She bit her lip, holding in a giggle when his mouth dropped open, and his eyes bulged. Then he threw his head back and laughed. "I should have known you'd take me to task sooner or later."

He stopped laughing and leaned closer. Her breath caught when his lips moved softly over hers. Once. Twice. If they hadn't been in public, the kiss might have deepened. Instead, it was a taste of their future.

The soft purr of Micah's car pulled up beside them.

"Let's go home, wife," Gideon said, his whisper husky, his breath warm against her cheek.

Home. New energy rushed through her. Together they made their way to Micah's waiting vehicle, ready to begin their future.

* * * * *

*If you enjoyed this book, don't miss
the other heart-stopping Amish adventures
from Dana R. Lynn's Amish Country Justice series:*

Available now from Love Inspired Suspense!

*Find more great reads at
www.LoveInspired.com.*

Dear Reader,

Thank you for joining me in the final book about the five Bender siblings. When we first met Gideon Bender, he was the energetic youngest brother and a practical joker. The more I thought about him, the more I began to appreciate how much depth his character had. He downplays his skills to blend in with his community. No one really understands him.

Except Beth. They used to be friends. Beth hasn't forgiven Gideon for ending their friendship. She needs to trust in him and in God in a way she never foresaw. I enjoyed helping them reconnect and strengthen their faith in God's plan.

Thank you for reading Gideon and Beth's journey! I hope you enjoyed it. I love connecting with readers. You can find me on Facebook, Instagram, Bookbub and at www.danarlynn.com. Consider signing up for my monthly newsletter for the latest book news.

Blessings,
Dana R. Lynn